SANCTUARY OF LIES

Chad Bishop

Sanctuary of Lies

Copyright © 2017

All rights reserved.

ISBN-13: 978 -1-948377-00-3

A book isn't just an author's words; it's the result of a journey. I want to thank God for being my comforter, my inspiration, and my strength.

And, E.G. for being honest, logical and most of all my friend

Sanctuary of Lies

by

Chad Bishop

CHAPTER ONE

Monday 7:30 a.m., Orlando

AUCTIONEER: Ladies and Gentlemen welcome to Sanctuary. The first item up for auction is the latest software from Safe Haven, Houdini. As you know, whoever controls the skies can effectively hold a country hostage within its borders. Houdini accomplishes that goal. Planes go through five phases: The tower gets them to the runway, at that time the plane is visible to those directing the plane at the airport. It's then handed off to the nearest Terminal Radar Approach Control Facilities or "TRACON" for those of you who are familiar with this process and goes into phase two. In phase two, TRACON can't see the plane. As the name suggests, it's directing the plane via radar screens. Once the plane gets off the ground and is on the flight path, it goes into phase three and handed off to center. Center gets the plane within the range of the receiving TRACON and when TRACON accepts the handoff phase four begins. The receiving TRACON hands it off to receiving Tower, and that is the final phase.

Houdini should be used during phase two or phase four for maximum effect. We've arranged a demonstration during phase four, so you can see Houdini in action. If you look at the screens located in the front and the back of the room, we'll begin.

Today was Marcus' birthday, and he would kill 416 people before lunch.

Marcus swiped his picture ID over the white card reader on the wall. He looked at it and smiled at a picture of himself with a wide grin and a short buzz cut. The day he got this job he went to a barber and asked for a sharp look. The barber was an ex-marine and gave Marcus the cut of a "real man." His birthday always made him reminisce.

Marcus worked in the Southern California Terminal Radar Approach Control Facilities otherwise known as TRACON. As a 5-year veteran, Marcus welcomed walking into the dark circular room on the fifth floor. The green glow of radar circles on monitors decorated the circumference. The concentrated chatter of other Air Traffic Controllers guiding planes safely into and out of the surrounding airports served as background hum that welcomed him into the room.

Marcus sat down at his station and nodded to the man next to him and began to review the screen. Five years had taught him patience. He'd start slow and ease into his eight-hour shift. On the upper right of the screen, he saw a green blip. Marcus clicked on it, and the handoff begins for him to land the plane.

"Approach at 14000 descending to 12000" SW3678

"Southwest 3678 Roger" Marcus said.

As the blip moved closer to the center of the radar, Marcus could see the plane heading for the waypoint Seaview2.

Marcus remembered when he had started his dream job, and the trainer had said let's talk about circles and stars. At first, Marcus had thought he was crazy, and that's why he's retiring, but later, he treasured all of the words of his mentor. He'd told him "When you see a circle that's a VOR, and it's a real radar on the ground. The VOR's (VHF omnidirectional radar) correlated to physical equipment on the ground. When you see a star, it's a waypoint that a logical point, and you'll be using them to help land the plane. Remember logical is code for not real. We have the stars in between VOR's so we can guide the planes with more precision." That day when he went home, and his kids had asked him what did he do, he said: "Daddy played with circles and stars on a screen and landed a plane."

Now the VOR's are being slowly phased out since FAA, (Federal Aviation Administration) mandated the use of the new ADS-B (Automatic Dependent Surveillance-Broadcasting) protocols.

ADBS Protocol would bring the planes in more efficiently. Marcus wasn't sure he bought into the FAA and their new protocol. The rumor was first FAA would make VOR's obsolete and then they would begin to do the same thing with Air Traffic Controllers. When the FAA guy had come to TRACON, he said some fancy mumbo "they would begin working with the Air Traffic

Controllers, on Limiting human intervention" for their sake of course.

SEAVIEW2 is a standard terminal arrival route. The plane was coming in from the east. Marcus just needed to guide it to PARADISE VOR then to the LAHAB waypoint and finally the gate waypoint which would put them on an ILSs approach. He'd done it a thousand times.

The plane was at 14000 feet and going 310 knots. Marcus would slow it down and bring the plane in. Marcus wanted the plane to come in as quickly as possible. He scanned the radar and saw there are two more planes coming in from the North and West, but he had some time. The planes are on the outer edge of the radar.

"Southwest 3678 proceed to PARADISE."

Reply: Proceed to PARADISE 3678

Looking at the other two arrivals, Marcus thought about which path to put them on. Returning to look at the blips on the radar, he calculated how he would land the planes and then formulated his next set of instructions.

"Southwest 3678 begin descent to one one thousand."

Reply: begin descent to one one thousand southwest 3678

"Southwest 3678 proceed direct to LAHAB."

Reply: Proceed direct to LAHAB southwest 3678

Marcus looked at the arriving flights from the north west and then back at the incoming flight from the east.

The blip was gone.

"Southwest 3678 repeat," Marcus said.

Reply: Proceed directly to LAHAB southwest 3678

The blip was gone. The pilot was still talking, but the blip was gone.

"Where is it?" Marcus murmured.

Marcus's supervisor came over and touched him on his shoulder.

"Marcus?" the supervisor asked

"Southwest 3678 is gone."

"What?" the supervisor replied.

Out of habit, Marcus took the handoff from a plane in the south.

Reply: approach Pan16 at 7000 descending to 6000

"Roger Pan 16"

Marcus didn't turn. "You heard SouthWest's reply, but it's not on the radar,"

"Southwest 3678 descend to 9000."

"What are you telling him to move for if you can't see it?", the supervisor demanded.

"I can slow the plane when it falls below 10000; then the plane will go from the 310 knots to 250 knots. At 250 knots the plane is moving about 4 miles a minute. That I can estimate their location at least."

"Southwest 3678 turn right heading 270 descend and maintain 7000."

Reply: turn right heading 270 descend and maintain 7000 southwest 3678

"Pan 16 proceeds directly to SEAL BEACH."

"What did you hit! Where is the plane?" the supervisor said frantically, hovering over Marcus's shoulder.

When Marcus looked at the screen where there was once no blip, there are now four, and all of them are labeled SW3678.

"Southwest 3678 descend and maintain 5000."

"What are you doing? They're already at 5000" the supervisor yelled.

Marcus ignored the supervisor and concentrated on the task at hand. Two planes are coming in from the northwest, one coming from the south and southwest 3678.

His supervisor called the man next to him, "Jim take the handoff in the northwest and Paul take Pan 16 in south."

"Southwest 3678 cleared ILS 25 left approach."

Marcus wiped the sweat from his brow as he watched all four blips approach runway 25L.

"Southwest 3678 are you on the frequency?"

There was nothing but crackle.

"Southwest 3678 contact the tower."

The blips started to ascend on the approach.

"No, no" Marcus whispered.

Just like it started, the plane began its descent, and there was only one blip on the screen for flight 3678.

"It's coming in too fast." Marcus murmured

Then the sounds of SouthWest came back on, and all they could hear are the cries of help from the aircraft.

Marcus didn't think "emergency vehicles to 25L, everyone calling standby."

AUCTIONEER: As you can see Houdini work. We'll

start the bidding at 45 million.
***

Headlines from the evening paper:
AIR TRAFFIC CONTROLLER CLAIMS SYSTEM
MALFUNCTION, 416 DEAD

CHAPTER TWO

Thursday 6:00 a.m., New York

Looking at your future wife in the bed and getting a text message from your dead
ex-wife are all of the makings of a bad day.

Jacob Costa returned his cell to the night table. Simone Johns has been dead for three days; she could wait a bit longer. Next, to him, Isabella Nunez, his fiancée, reached for him.

"Jake?" she murmurs sleep muffling her voice. Bella is a treasure. She is as subtle as a freight truck when it comes to her emotions and is as brilliant as a mad scientist. He didn't answer her if he did they'd both be in bed for another hour. It is time for him to get out of bed, go to work, and reply to his dead ex.

Jacob turns onto his back and listens to the dark of their condo. He takes inventory of his surroundings before he moves. Bella has already fallen back to sleep, her snoring signaling her retreat. Jacob listens to the birds chirping in front of the living room window, the faucet dripping in their adjacent bathroom, and so on. When all the sounds are accounted for, Jacob swings his legs over the side of the bed. If nothing else, foster care had taught him to assess his surroundings before he moves. You only have one opportunity to surprise the enemy.

He thought about looking at the text but, stops himself. He won't let Simone upset his schedule. Necessities must be done first, and then he could handle the trials of the day. Worrying never solved a problem. By following a daily regimen, he has more time to think, and it lets the enemy worry over the silence.

Jacob walks to the bathroom and begins his morning routine: go to the bathroom, close the door behind him, confirm the door is closed, shower, towel off, brush his teeth, and then wipe down the sink.

He exits the bathroom to find Bella looking at him with her leg thrown over the top sheet. Her legs are phenomenal. Jacob takes a second to appreciate the view before he turns on the television to the news channel.

Jacob smiles to himself when he hears her sigh of frustration. If Bella knew he was teasing her, she'd return in kind. After Simone, he didn't think he'd run into a woman he could understand. Other women are interested in what he had or where he was going. Bella just wants him. More importantly, Bella is his best friend. Now that didn't mean Bella didn't have her faults, but she owns them. For Simone, she always had the "we should get them before they got us" mentality. The text is probably anything but good.

"Are you hungry?" he asks as he looks over his shoulder. Jacob sees Bella's brows go up and her smile transforms her into a mischievous minx. She throws the covers off her body to reveal a very naked Bella.

"Funny you should ask. I woke up hungry, but you had already gone into the shower." Bella replies.

Jacob cares for Bella. It wasn't the stuff of fairy tales that he was told about, Jacob doesn't do Prince Charming. To Jacob, caring meant he would see to her needs, be there when she needs it and protect her. Jacob never claimed to be romantic, but he is committed. It hadn't been enough for Simone, but it seems like Bella will take him as he is and not hope for him to change like so many women hope after marriage.

Bella is curvy and is about 5'6 tall. She is tall enough for him to find her in a crowd and she has a laugh that is loud and infectious.

'Simone's text message would steal some of Bella's joy, and it has to be handled' he thinks to himself as he dresses for the day.

"It's time to make the donuts, so you're going to have to hold out until tonight. If you want food, I can take you to the diner on my way to work." Jacob replies as he picks up his phone and reviews the text messages again. It was the same. Six messages from new clients, four messages on updated projects, one unknown text, and Simone Johns.

"Hey, what's wrong?" Bella asks as she sits up and pulls the sheet over her chest.

"I don't know yet. When I know, I'll tell you." Jacob answers as he hooks his phone in its holster on his hip.

"I just want you to know I'm here if you need me," Bella says with a forced smile.

It is moments like these that Jacob is grateful for Bella. She didn't nag or whine. She let him think, and when he is ready, he could tell her. The concern in her eyes and her hands clenching on the sheet are a dead giveaway on how hard it is for her not to ask any other questions. He turns to walk out the bedroom when he is stopped by Bella's voice.

"Hey! Where are my kisses?! If you're not going to feed me, I should get kisses at the very least!" she said with a pout.

Jacob walks to the bed and Bella meets him at the edge. She throws her arms around him and smiles.

"Come closer, you know so that I can kiss you better." she teases.

He leans in, and Bella pulls him into a deep kiss. He feels her leaning back, trying to pull him onto the bed. Jacob brakes the kiss and smiles at her.

"I've got work, and no matter how big you think you are, the truth is I'm still bigger than you."

Bella falls back on the bed. "Fine, go I'll go pick up our baby and meet you later."

"I don't know how you can call a 60 lb. Bluenose Pit Bull a baby but, okay." Jacob says as he shakes his head. He looks at his watch, gives Bella another kiss and then leaves their condo.

The August morning was bright, and the heat is already starting to rise. He steps into his black car and pushes the engine start button. The car starts its system, and the A/C begins to cool the car. Jacob pulls his phone out and taps Simone's text:

Hello Jake,

I'll get straight to the point. I've been murdered, and I need you to protect our son.

Your response is required.

Jacob closes the text and re-holsters the phone.

"Sending texts from the grave, that's got to be one for the books."

CHAPTER THREE

Thursday 6:00 a.m., Orlando at Sanctuary

'Digging graves in a golf course is not as easy as it looks' thought John Kooma. He stands up as the cool Florida morning wind dries the sweat from his soaked work shirt. A pair of chipmunks stop a foot away, turn, and run away. He should be used to it by now. It isn't like this is the first body he'd put here.

Watching the chipmunks retreat he thought 'Look at that, even animals have enough sense not to be nosy.' John reaches into his back pocket and pulls out a bottle of spring water. After taking a large gulp from the bottle, he wipes his mouth and looks at the grave in front of him.

'It sure is a shame she had to go. At least she won't be alone. I've buried the other five in this same area so you all can talk to each other if you need to. I think being nosy is a sin, so you might not be making it to the Lord anytime soon but, you'll have each other.'

John looks at the other new grass plugs in the area. He is a tidy man. He always cleans up after himself. After picking up his shovel, he continues to even the ground. Then, just like so many before her, he put the grass plugs over them. When he is done he notices he hadn't brought the water cans, so he just empties his bottle of water over her plot. It isn't enough water, but he knows he'll be back, there are always nosy people.

At 6'1 John is a simple man. He has simple taste, and he runs a simple organization. He doesn't speak much, and he keeps to himself. He understood, from an early age, that his appearance doesn't inspire people. In fact, a lot of people can't even recall meeting him much less describe him, and that is okay with John.

He isn't one of those who manages from behind a desk. John spends a majority of his time in the field, so much so a lot of his subordinates don't even know what he looks like. He's been in this business for 26 years. He is getting tired, and lately, John thinks about simply walking away. He has more than enough money and investments. When he leaves, he knows someone will step into his spot. The simple man wants a simple life. Technology is getting ahead of him.

Every couple of months, Miss Jane will come by. She'll give him updates and help him pass the time. The only thing she wants is for him to give her the monthly reports. John doesn't mind the exchange. The intimate time he spends with Miss Jane more than makes up for her attitude. Jane is like the rest of them, they don't see him, and they all think they can use him and go. Slow doesn't mean dumb. Miss Jane is simpler than him; she just doesn't know it.

John walks across the golf course, and he sees the beginning of the crowds coming on the course. He doesn't understand why they need to come out 6 am every morning to hit a little white ball across a green lawn. John's thinking is that the game is too easy. 'Hitting a ball into a non-moving target is as easy as sniping a man coming out of the grocery store. There doesn't seem to be a lot of skill involved in that at all. They just need to control their breathing and have patience, something every rookie assassin knows.'

No one notices him as he crosses the greens. One or two of the guests give him a look of strained patience, but when they look at his blue workman overalls and the word 'Sanctuary' printed on it, they shake their heads and turn away.

John has been staking out Sanctuary for months. Now, when he looks at the people who live here they all look alike to him: expendable. The couple coming on the field reminds him of the first couple he buried in the grove. That couple had been rich. Both women waved their hands around thinking they could command everyone around them. The dead couple had come to his place saying they needed maintenance. When John told them someone would come, she pushed her way into his home, and the husband followed. John had to kill them then. Fortunately, they were visiting and not employees on Sanctuary. That is the challenge of working on Sanctuary, the employees of Safe Haven lived in the community.

John walks to the community center and sees a well-toned male at the desk. He is an agent. This guy reminds John of his third kill in the grove. Another agent had come to the community of Sanctuary. John couldn't tell if the man at the desk is a government guy or a consultant, but he could tell he is the business. The agent had a slim body that came from use, not from a gym.

The third guy in the grove had been a freelancer. He had explained to John this job was big enough for the both of them. John is a simple man, not a sharing man. John knows Simone Johns has created the Houdini and it is possible that it is here. He is going to be the owner of that software.

John knows he isn't the smartest, but he is strong. He grew up on a farm where he discovered how to endure pain and how to live. His lanky frame gives people a false sense of comfort and hides a killer waiting to strike.

Finally, John arrives at the golf house and stares at the agent at the counter. John doesn't have time to bury another body today. He has just enough time to do the garbage run. He'll arrive at Ms. Johns house by 9:15. Just in time to see 8-year old David Johns come out to play. Miss Jane told him to watch the boy and be his friend if he could.

Ms. Jane also told John to be prepared to snatch David or kill him. Then she gave John some "assistance" with his other "needs." The fact that she isn't sure if they will kill or kidnap the boy told him the situation isn't under control. Miss Jane is a giving woman when she wants to be, but if things don't turn in the right direction he would have a talk with Ms. Jane, and she'll need to explain who she works for. John is a simple man, and he could wait.

He'll snatch the boy if need be, get his money, and then deal with Miss Jane and her employer, Mr. Carstairs. Maybe, Mr. Carstairs needs a gift to motivate him to find the Houdini software and deliver it to him.

CHAPTER FOUR

Recruitment ~ 9 years earlier

21 minutes to go time.

Who doesn't like chocolate? Simone wonders as she sits parked in her van on William Street in New York. The small side street is filling with other vans that are making routine deliveries to the busy enclave. Like most streets in downtown Manhattan, it is filled with too many cars in too little of space. She is sitting in a white truck with her foot on the dashboard. It is the thrill of hunting in the big city that gets her going. She can be hunting a big deal, or she can be hunting data, like today.

It is 11: 40, 20 minutes to go.

The meter maid has already passed by twice, but Simone knows her license plate is current and it is registered as a commercial vehicle. Besides, what kind of man took a job as a meter maid? He can just keep walking his round self on down the block until he finds some unsuspecting newbie, who doesn't know the rules in the area and doesn't have an old ticket in the window.

The reason she is here is that of a man named Justin Whatley. Justin is a complete ass. A 5'10, ivy league graduate with amazing hair, and a smile that had most women ready to have his children, but an ass nonetheless. He works for the Federal Trade Commission and as far as anyone can tell he can't be bought. Not because he is ethical. He can't be bought because he is so narcissistic that no one has enough money to feed his over-inflated ego. Of course, coming from old money helps him keep to the moral high road.

She looks at her clock on her wrist, 11:50.

At the ripe age of 25, Justin Watley has been gifted a job via his dad's connections to work in the FTC. In his sweaty palms, rests information that can make or break a company. Simone is known for making good calls when it comes to innovative technology and companies, but Justin is a loose cannon, who doesn't know how to follow the logic. The last two companies she has picked, Justin has doomed their initial outlooks by expressing that he 'hadn't made a final decision.'

FTC doesn't have to say there is a problem. Justin only has to dramatically pause when asked about the company and then he says, "We'll see...," To doom a company's prospects. He never has to retract a statement because dramatic pauses don't count, but the damage has been done and the woman with the 'Midas Touch,' Simone Johns, is in jeopardy of losing her place in the tech world as being an Oracle.

Simone learned early, in the real-world men got three strikes and women who are MENSA members, genius' and have six-figure incomes, receive three strikes as well. It is all equal in its own way.

It is 11:55, time to prepare.

Desperate times call for desperate actions. Simone has taken two weeks' vacation after the last two misses. Everyone at her job thinks she is burnt out and is going to come back announcing her need to leave the company. Even Jacob, the love of her life, asked her to take some time and relax. Jacob's answer is "This will pass." and "We have enough money to be comfortable."

'Comfortable is for the good guys,' Simone thought. When you are a good guy, comfortable means a good life. When you aren't part of the boys' club, comfortable means working as an assistant and doing the work for the good guys.

Fortunately, Justin has a vice. He loves to take notes on his phone about the new rules that he has just heard and makes notes to himself on the decisions he'll vote for. He doesn't believe in paper notes, and while some people think he is playing games on his phone, a very high paid companion confirms, he likes to brag about his notes. The woman confirms that he thinks it is fitting for him to write to himself about what is going on, besides who else can understand his genius but him.

Simone knows with certainty, he actually writes on his phone and keeps the information to review. That is all she needed to come up with a plan to make sure she doesn't strike out a third time.

Finally, it is noon.

Simone picks up the Pringles can on the floor and removes the top. Inside, there is a wire setup, so she can find an open wi-fi for her to ride the signal. Why bring your own when you can use someone else's? She steps out of the truck and stretches with her Pringles can in hand. When the meter maid comes by she nods again, and he grimaces at her. There are those who do something in life and those who endure. The meter maid is a warning to those who endure.

She turns the can upside and puts it on top of the van. She stretches her neck and then gets back into the van. She opens her laptop and searches for a signal. When she finds a signal, she runs some simple searches with a lot of return rows to make sure it will hold.

The FTC is still using windows 7. She types the command to scan for devices. She did this on Day Two to retrieve the MAC address of the phone. That's when she discovered the MAC address of the phone would change daily when he disconnects from the network. Her strategy now is to make a small jammer for the phone and make it disconnect. When the phone disconnects, it will go into "advertisement" mode. When it goes into that mode, she will be able to identify the mac address of the phone and gain entry. After she has the address, she will have a small window to download the notes. Justin likes to review his notes before lunch. There are two computer companies waiting for an FTC judgment. The coding community wonders if the FTC would single out one company from the other as being too intrusive. If she can call this decision, she'd be back on top.

It is 12:15.

Justin is eating lunch. He will put his phone away, and eat uninterrupted like the king he is. She types in the command on her machine and waits. In minutes, the memos from his machine download. She scans them, quickly finding the company she is looking for and laughs. Simone turns off her computer, puts it back in the case, and then steps out of the van. She retrieves the Pringles can from the roof and gets back in the van.

"Hello, Ms. Johns."

She jumps when she saw the man sitting in the seat next to her. "Who are you and what are you doing in my van?"

"Ms. Johns or should I call you Simone. My name is Sean Carstairs, and I represent a firm called Nova Enterprises. I'm the owner and Head of Recruitment, and I think we have a lot to offer one another."

"I'm going to be offering up a scream if you don't get out of my van!"

The man laughs and sits back in his seat. "You could do that, but then I would have to tell Mr. Whatley about your little habit of looking at his notes."

Simone sits back and waits. "Who are you and what do you want?"

"I want us to make a lot of money Ms. Johns, let's go somewhere and talk about our future."

CHAPTER FIVE

Thursday 9:00 a.m., Orlando

Peter must decide if it is better to keep his son and
risk his life or give his son up and give himself a chance
at living longer. Peter looks at the email from Jacob
Costa and clenches his teeth. He knew this moment was
coming. Still, he isn't prepared. His hands curl into fists
on the wooden desk.

Peter has everything. He lives in a house, in a
community he and Simone had built. The community is
called Sanctuary and, for eight years, it had been theirs.
They also owned Safe Haven Company, one of the most
profitable toy companies on the East Coast. Still, that
isn't enough to stop this day from happening.

He looks at the little boy on the hardwood floor
playing with his truck. The office walls are decorated
with shelves of computer hardware on one wall and the
other wall has paintings from Matisse to Goya. The

room is as eclectic as the couple who used to sit here every evening and discuss how to keep the world at bay.

The desk has three items on it, the laptop he is using and two pictures. On the right is a picture of David on the bow of the boat called the 'Chariot.' Simone had purchased the boat for David. Peter told her it was too much, but she dismissed him as she always did when it came to spoiling David.

David's dark hair is blowing in the wind, and his smile is so big you could see his missing front teeth. His eyes looked like little slits instead of the large brown orbs of curiosity Peter saw every morning. In David's hand, he had a tiny replica of the Chariot. Like most things, David wished for it, and Simone gave it to him.

On the other side of the desk is a picture of him. Peter doesn't particularly like it, but he doesn't particularly like pictures at all. It is an old picture. It was the day he had passed the bar exam. He had been young then. A young black man who thought he was going to make a difference in the world. He had on a cheap suit that he had bought with his first paycheck as a junior law partner. His eyes are bright and full of hope for the future. He has a bigger body now, and no one would mistake him for that idealistic boy in the picture. Prison has a way of changing a person.

He closes the laptop and looks at David.

"Daddy what's wrong?" asks David.

Three days ago, he lost Simone, and now he is going to lose his son. He knows Jacob will answer. Simone

told him enough about Jacob. The both of them knew
what would happen. Peter is the one who sent the email
as soon as the police told him Simone's car had been
found down the ditch.

There is no time to waste. The only thing that
mattered is David.

"Nothing is wrong David; everything is going the
way it's supposed to," Peter replies.

The 8-year old boy stops and pushes a hank of dark
hair out of his face. "If everything is okay why are you
frowning?"

Peter smiles. "You're just like your mother."

David smiles showing off two missing teeth in the
front. "You only say that when I'm in trouble. Ms. Wise
will take care of us."

Peter tries to step carefully around the subject of Ms.
Wise. It has only been three days since Simone's death,
and the child psychologist has said David will try to
deal with this in his way. Peter should be prepared for
David to manifest imaginary friends. These things will
come from his inability to accept her death. Hearing it
is one thing, but being with David and experiencing it is
another.

In the last three days, according to David, Ms. Wise
has become his new best friend. Ms. Wise has been one
of the first toys Simone bought when they came to
Sanctuary. Peter understood why the boy gravitated to
the toy, but that doesn't make it any easier to deal with.

"David, we talked about Ms. Wise remember? She's
your favorite toy, but toys aren't real like people. They

don't really talk." David pulls Ms. Wise, the stuffed owl, to his chest and nods.

"Yeah, I 'member." David mumbles.

Peter sits down next David and pulls him into an embrace. David relaxes into his embrace and clutches Ms. Wise even tighter to his chest. Peter considered not sending the email, but they are out of options. Obligations must be fulfilled. Simone had said it would be the final deal with Nova and the beginning of our freedom.

The product hadn't been delivered, and 85 million dollars had gone missing. These aren't the kind of customers who just walked away. They would ransom David for the money, or they'd kill him to make a statement to others who don't deliver. Neither option is acceptable.

Peter takes a breath and rises to answer the email. The email wasn't about him, this is all for David and making sure he stays alive.

CHAPTER SIX

Friday 9:00 a.m., Orlando Airport

Hell wanted its due, and the collector is his lover, Isabella.

"The foolishness of men never ceases to amaze me." Isabella declares.

"Where are we going, Bella?" Jacob asks.

"I'm going to pick up my baby before we go see yours." She snips.

Jacob doesn't say anything. If Justice makes her feel better, he is all for it. They pick up Justice from the terminal then, settle Justice in the back seat of the rental truck. The drive to the hotel is a silent affair, and the tension builds with every mile. By the time they arrive at the hotel, getting out of the car is a necessity.

Bella takes Justice out of the truck, leaving Jacob behind. He closes the door and watches Bella strut to the hotel counter with Justice on what they affectionately called "the kiddie leash." He arrives just in time to hear the front desk clerk speak.

"We have pet sitting services if you'd like?" the front desk clerk offers a cheery smile.

"No."

" Yes." Jacob and Isabella answer in unison. To their credit, the front desk person waits for the confusion to settle and their smile doesn't falter once.

Then Jacob speaks again. "Yes, her name is Justice, and we'll pick her up later today."

The front desk person nods. Bella grabs her room key and walks off as Jacob finishes signing the paperwork and brings the bags.

Bella isn't prone to emotional flares but, when she did have them, they need to be addressed.

* * *

The hotel is clean, and the air is cool. When Jacob walks into the hotel room, there is a bathroom on the immediate right. As he walks down the hall, it opens into a sitting area with striped wallpaper, a brown couch and a desk on the opposite wall. Bella is sitting at the desk. Isabella's legs are crossed, and the top leg is rocking back and forth. Jacob knows if he gets close enough she'll probably kick him. It's almost worth it to break the tension.

Jacob swears he could hear her temper rising. He leans against the wall and waits.

"I told you I would come here, find the truth and then address the situation," Jacob starts.

"What does that mean, exactly?" Isabella asks.

"It means we gather the facts, analyze the situation

and then make an informed decision," Jacob replies.

"This isn't some work project. You have to – "Isabella begins.

"Stop. Until we know something, this is exactly what I'll do. You know me, I don't move until I understand what's going on." Jacob replies.

"There's a "but" in there Jake. And that's the problem. Your good nature is great most of the time, but Simone is using it from the grave, and our lives are being tossed into the air."

"You know me, Bella, so what's bothering you? Say it and let's move past it."

Isabella gets up and stops in front of him. She is close enough for him to see her bottom lip tremble and the glassiness of tears in her eyes.

"Move past it? We can't move past it ever! She left you a son who is the sole heir to a multi-million-dollar company! Everybody knows the company, Safe Haven! How can I compete with that, Jake?"

"Bella?" Jacob asks incredulously.

"Fine! I'm not worried about the money. But a son? The only child I'll ever be able to give you is Justice."

She turns to darts to the bedroom.

"Bella," Jacob calls.

"Whatever Jake," she tosses over her shoulder. "I don't want to hear it anyway. You're going to be the noble knight and do you, and I'm going to be the side chick to a dead woman."

Jacob follows Isabella and puts his hand on the door right before it slams in his face. He pushes it back open.

Bella stands in front of the bed with her hands on her hips, ready for a fight.

"You know me. I'm not a boy. I don't do hysterics. I don't let emotion make decisions. I have to do what I can live with."

Isabella's hands drop, and she takes a step towards Jacob.

"I know that. I also know that sometimes the good guys get screwed. I'm selfish enough to say it. I don't want to wait or sacrifice to have a relationship with you. I thought we are at a good place and I see it all crumbling."

"Do you think I'm a wishy-washy person?"

Isabella shakes her head.

"Then breathe. I'm going to do what has to be done. Trust me." Jacob says.

Bella frowns. "Your son is making my issues flare up, and I'm not sure how to get through it."

"I can deal with your issues Bella. Just like you deal with mine."

Bella raises her eyebrows. "Yeah, your issues are pretty bad."

"Bella, I've seen your issues. It's not as a bad as you think. Are we done with this conversation?'

She looks over her shoulder to see the bed and turns to him.

"Do you think this will solve anything?"

Jacob pulls her into his embrace and kisses her.

"No, but I think it will help you to remember, we're a team, Bella."

She steps back into his arms and pulls him to the bed. As Jacob takes off his clothes and places them on the dresser, Isabella throws off her clothes and lays bare on the bed. With arms open, a smile on her face, soft skin, and an eager body, this is Bella. She is needy and reaffirming at the same time. Jacob watches her closely as he brings her to several peaks.

Her body is bathed in sweat, and she holds nothing back from him. Jacob frames her face and watches her as they both shudder and lay gasping after the moment. Isabella curls into his side, and Jacob kisses her forehead as she dozes. Jacob lays in the hotel bed and runs scenarios in his head on how he will make sure his family will be safe.

CHAPTER SEVEN

Negotiations ~ 9 years ago
Simone knows a con man when she sees him. It doesn't
matter if they are trolling the streets of Brooklyn where she
grew up or dressed in expensive clothes like Sean Carstairs.
They all have beady little eyes and predatory smiles.
"What do you want Sean Carstairs?"
Sean's smile grew wider, and Simone starts calculating
where she could run and how she will explain this to Jacob.
The van feels small. Her mother had always told her not to
take her eyes off a snake, and today she is facing the largest
one she'd ever seen.
"I hear you're the woman with the 'Midas touch.' I've been
watching you. I thought it was just dumb luck. Imagine my
surprise to find you actually have a brain in that pretty
package. I believe in making opportunities, Simone. My
company needs someone like you."
"Like me? You need me to give them classes on how to
make antennas from Pringles cans? Or we could go hi-tech,

and I could show them how to do it from a coffee can. Fewer parts to make you know."

He laughs and sits back in the van facing forward. "Let's go for a drive, Simone."

"No, I don't think so. I may not have a lot of choices in life, but I'll choose when and how I die. You want to kill me; you can do it here."

He looks at her and then reaches into his pocket and pulls out a picture of Jacob.

"He's a fine-looking man. What is it? Two almost three years you two been married? I have no intention of killing you. I think we can both agree. Jacob isn't like us. He still believes in rules. I don't, and I think you're the same otherwise why would you be here in front of the FTC building?"

"Using blackmail to get a person's cooperation is tacky and extreme for a first meeting. It doesn't bode well for me trusting you. But you've done your research Mr. Carstairs so, for now, you've got my attention. Without a clue on what you want from me, I'm not moving this van. What do you want?"

"Ever play in the dark web Simone?"

"You mean the black market?"

"No, I mean the dark web where real sales happen and where everything is for sale. We have people who look for talented problem solvers like you to create quick solutions for people who can't afford not to have a solution. The world is changing, and we need to accommodate the need." Sean explains.

"If you want a hacktivist. I don't 'problem solve' for a cause. Whatever I do, I do for money and profit. I'm talented

but female. The tech game is a short-term, high return game for me. I'll get but so far in this market, and then I'll cap out. If your team is made up of other like-minded industry males, I may not be an addition you want."

"That might have been true once upon a time Simone but, as of today you've just been promoted to running the boys' tech club."

"You think you have enough pull to do that?" Simone asks sarcastically.

"In my world, yes. Forget about corporate Simone. Let me show you a place where skill and results are the only things that matter."

"If I say no, then what? We'll be right where we started."

"No Simone. If you say no, it will be the beginning of the end of Jacobs career. He's a good guy who wants to do things the right way. I can make him a pariah. Besides that, I'd be disappointed in you. Saying no would go against everything I've learned about you. Decide Simone, come listen to the rest of my proposal or watch your husband get ostracized from the only thing he's ever done."

Simone turns the engine and then turns to Sean.

"I'm going with you because I want to see if you can do what you say you can do. But remember, today you have the upper hand, it won't always be this way, and I'm very patient." Simone promises.

"I'll remember that now drive we have money to make," Sean says with a smile.

CHAPTER EIGHT

Friday 9:00 a.m., Orlando at Nova headquarters

Jane Smith would be a good team member if you didn't mind watching your back all the time. She's the type that could justify eating one of her offspring if she had at least one left. The thing to remember is to shoot first and ask questions later. When Jane strides into Sean's office, he opens the desk drawer and puts his hand on his gun just in case.

"Jane, progress?" Sean asks nonchalantly.

She sits down in one of the two matching sitting chairs to the right of his desk. Jane crosses her long legs, one over the other, making the black pencil skirt inch up her legs. She runs her hand through her blond-streaked hair and gives him a long sigh.

"Have you forgotten how to use your words, Jane?" Sean asks sarcastically.

"If I had anything I would have come in or reported it. It's a waste of both of our time for you to request a meeting. When I have something, I'll let you know," Jane replies.

"This project is time sensitive dear. And I have to say your check-ins are usually more frequent than they have been for this project."

Sean sees Jane look at him and he knows what she sees. He isn't looking like his normal organized self. His shirt is buttoned crooked, his tie isn't knotted exact, and his coat looks like it has a crease in it.

"What's wrong?" she asks.

"Did I say there was?" Sean replies, annoyed.

"Sean, cut it! Tell me the problem, or you can call in one of your other 'employees' to play cat and mouse games with you." Jane snaps. She sounds firm and in control, but he could tell from the slight warble in her voice that she isn't as composed as she seems. Jane hasn't liked this project from the very beginning. She warned him when feelings get involved; people start to die. Sean explained away her reticence as a lack of courage. He hasn't looked at how focused he was on getting Simone and as a result had wound up making a deal with a madman.

Sean closes the draw and sits back in his chair. "It's funny you should bring up games that people play. Look on the credenza it seems the office received a present this morning."

Jane stands, bewilderment on her face. Sean is relieved that Jane is lost and at the same time terrified. If Jane doesn't know about this, that meant he is running out of time. Jane walks to the cherry wood credenza located directly across from her seat. She sees the white rectangular box. She looks back over her shoulder.

Sean nods for her to continue. "Please continue, I want to share the joyful experience."

She opens the box and inside is a cake. It is a rectangular cake with white and red flowers on the border of the cake. In the middle of the cake is red writing that said, 'I'm watching you.' After the red script writing on the cake, two human eyeballs are inserted after the phrase. Jane takes a small breath and then closes the lid.

"As you can see, our buyer isn't as patient as he made it seem last week."

"Those are green eyes, that means ..."

"It means Miranda no longer has hers and she probably doesn't need them now anyway," Sean explains.

"Have you had the cake and delivery – "

Sean cuts her off with an upraised hand. "This isn't a television show. I don't care how it got here Jane. I know who it came from. The message is clear, we don't have time, and the client is either on his way or sending a representative. Where are we with finding the merchandise or the money?"

"I'm looking. There have been no new players on site. I've got a person watching the boy."

"One of ours?"

"No."

"No? Are you subcontracting – "

"Sean, I'm not. I used what was available. He's a simpleton at the site. He works for Sanctuary; he's a groundskeeper. He's a little slow, but he notices everything."

Sean laughs. "Ah yes, Jane, you are so dependably treacherous. No one is exempt from the game."

Jane stands up and walks to the door and says over her shoulder. "When the game is worth 85 million dollars everyone is in the game."

Sean sees her exit and looks at the box. Maybe he'd remove the eyes and give it to his staff, no sense in wasting the cake.

CHAPTER NINE

Friday 10:00 a.m., Orlando at Nova headquarters

Being loyal is a good trait, but living is a better one.

Jane Smith knows the dynamics of the game have just changed and it is time to find out who is going to be the winner. As she walks out of the professional office, done in muted blue and grays, she thinks about how everything you know can change in a heartbeat. Earlier this week, Sean Carstairs was in control. Two days later, he has lost his product, his money, and the person he had on a leash is dead. Jane doesn't like coincidences, and there are too many happening against Sean. It is time to re-evaluate her position. She walks down the hall and pulls out her phone.

"John?"

"Jane, is that you?"

She rolls her eyes. John is a necessary evil. Jane grew up in a small town that had one stoplight, three businesses, and one hotel. None of those options appealed to her. She worked the hotel for a week, took the money, and got on a bus to the nearest city. You wouldn't know it, but Jane has two degrees: one in accounting and one in business. She tried going straight, but she realizes that there is an unbalance in the world when it came to the sexes. If she is going to have to work for a man she wanted to maximize her time because she realized her looks also played into the equation.

If Jane's mother were any indication she isn't always going to be tall, athletic and statuesque, time would take its toll. Her blond hair will thin sooner than later, and strands of gray already decorated her head. Her prominent cheekbones will wind up being the scaffolding for hollowing cheeks and deep lines around her mouth. Time is of the essence, money needs to be made, and it has to be invested wisely and discreetly.

Sean Carstairs thinks he saved her. He pays well, and he doesn't ask questions about her off time. Sometimes she'll drive by the old town. Her mother has already passed, but her sister has two kids and lives in the same town. Jane's sister lives the fate she had avoided. Still, Jane respects her sister for staying and trying to make it work. Jane set up two college funds for the kids and every two months a wad of money appears under her sister's pillow. It isn't much, but it is as much as Jane would do.

"Yes John, it's me. I want to know if there is any activity?"

"There was some activity but, I won't know for a

couple of days."

"I'll be there soon, so we can talk about what's going on and what to look for," she says in a slow cadence. Jane wants to make sure John understands what she is saying.

"I miss you when you aren't here. Your company makes the time pass by." John says in a sing-song voice that reminds her to talk slow, so she doesn't lose John in a conversation.

"It's the same for me, John. I'll talk to you later" Jane replies.

She hangs up the phone and gets into her car. She drives around the city until she finally parks her car in a twenty-four-hour parking spot. She gets out of the car and opens the trunk. She pins her blonde hair up and pulls on a black bob wig, changes into a peasant shirt with blue jeans, and slips on hi-top sneakers.

She doesn't exit through the front. Instead, she walks down the staircase until she gets to the basement. She follows the basement to an underpass that goes into the building next door. The building next door is a school for beauty consultants. As a consultant herself, Jane thinks the term is so funny. The school trains hairdressers and manicurists. Before she exits the connecting tunnel, she puts on a jacket that is given to all beauty school students, and she leaves the building.

She is always cautious.

The cake is the beginning of the end. Sean doesn't realize it, but he is losing control. Not delivering to the simple man is as good as signing a death warrant.

The simple man could have been regulated to an urban myth if it wasn't for the bodies that showed up when he isn't happy. Sean doesn't have a plan. He is making it up as he goes. That means it is time to go looking for a new employer and to put some distance between her and the employer she has now. She'll visit John first and see if there is any profit to be made. If not, she'll leave and save herself.

CHAPTER TEN

Friday 11:30 a.m., Orlando going to Sanctuary

His woman is content, and Justice is happy in doggie daycare. Now it is time to find out if he has a son. A yellow cab waits in front of the hotel. He walks to the cab and gets in.

"Sanctuary Community," Jacob tells the driver.

"Me be knowing where you are goin'. I'm thinkin' we need to talk though," the driver says. Jacob shakes his head and leans back.

"I just can't get a break in this town," Jacob murmurs.

"Now, now Mr. Costa. I'm thinkin' we can talk on the way and maybe take the tourist path." The driver suggests.

"Okay, who are you? I just got here. I can't tell you anything because I don't know anything. You should have been a little more patient and waited until I came out of the meeting I'm going to." Jacob explains.

The cabbie laughs. Jacob looks at the man driving and

waits.

"Don't look at this bald head and thick accent and think I'm a little short on the smarts. I want you to know I work for the United States. You, Mr. Costa, are causing a lot of uproars. There aren't a lot of people like me at my level who think you should live. By the way, I'm not here to get information; I'm here to give it."

Jacob sits up with that bit of information.

"My name is Mr. Knight. I knew Simone. We had some dealings. She wasn't the best woman, but she was patriotic. A complicated gal, if ever I met one," Knight recalls.

"Then you've met Simone. Can you go back to the part where people want to kill me?"

Knight laughs. "It's nice to know you're listening."

"Who forgets when someone wants to kill them?!" Jacob asks sarcastically.

"It's not an issue for you now. Like I said I'm rooting for you." Mr. Knight reminds him.

"So, what are you going to tell me?" Jacob asks.

"I don't know what Peter is going to tell you. You are going to see Peter, right?"

Jacob smiles and nods. "I'm glad you're up to date on my calendar."

"I'm trying to serve the people."

"You are saying what about Simone, Peter and telling me something I don't already know?" Jacob urges.

Mr. Knight takes a deep sigh, stops at a light and then makes a turn going onto a four-lane highway.

"So, let me tell you the short story. A long time ago

the Department of defense built something called the onion router or as it was known then TOR. It disguised the person who was on it and let them travel incognito on the web. As with all geek moments, no one thought about how it would evolve they just wanted to be the first to create something new. Now people can use a Tor browser and enter what is called the Dark Web. On the dark web, a new economy was born, and it has several advantages and disadvantages. But there are enough advantages that the government keeps a presence on the web but can't regulate it anymore. When there is some unique software or chatter that seems interesting, we have people who let us know and if necessary act on our behalf. Simone was one of those people."

Jacob looks at the highway cars pass by. This was Simone. She wanted the big win, to be in the driver's seat and she played in a pond where there were bigger sharks than her.

"Why don't you just kill it? You made Tor, turn it off."

"Well as with all little monsters, they grow up. When we talk about dark web, we don't just mean Tor anymore. We mean any site that any common search engine can't find them. We affectionately call them darknets. Tor was one, and they spawned over so many other nets that we couldn't shut it down if we wanted to. Besides you'd be amazed at the legal firepower, they have."

"So, you're Frankenstein got away from you?" Jacob asks.

Mr. Knight shrugs. "It happens, more so than people want to know. Simone understood these things."

"If she understood so much and you had an agreement, why is she dead?"

"Simone was a smart girl, but she liked to build things, just because. One of her pet projects was put on the market. The FAA has mandated a new protocol be put on all commercial planes. Simone's project could interfere with the protocol and cause a disruption. She wasn't a team player."

"Why didn't you ask her for the antidote. She was curious but always responsible." Jacob counters.

"She was working on it, but then someone stole the code and put it up for auction. It sold for 85 million dollars, and we were out of time," Mr. Knight replies.

"Who bought it?"

"We don't know." Mr. Knight states through clenched teeth.

"And Simone's death? Do you know who did that?" Jacob asks.

"I can't say." Mr. Knight replies.

Jacob pauses and looks at Mr. Knights eyes reflecting in the rear-view mirror.

"You can't say isn't the same as a no."

"Well, I can't say is all I can give you." Knight deflects.

"Was the code delivered?'

"No," says Knight.

"Where is the code?" Jacob asks as a sinking feeling starts to settle in his gut.

"We don't know."

"Tell me you at least know if the money was delivered?"

Mr. Knight doesn't answer. Jacob can see Mr. Knight's hands tighten on the wheel as he drives.

"Okay so let me get this straight. You've got a missing program that can screw up all the commercial planes in the sky. You don't know who tried to buy it. You don't have the money, and you don't have the code. Is that right?" Jacob askes.

Mr. Knight nods his head curtly.

Jacob laughs. "Then take me back to the hotel. I don't want to set foot on Sanctuary. I'll call Peter, and we will handle our business elsewhere."

"I'm afraid that's not an option either." Mr. Knight begins.

Jacob looks at Mr. Knight and sighs heavily. "On Simone's death, several documents are delivered."

"And?" Jacob replies.

"Simone sent one to me with a copy of the one she sent to you and an additional note."

"Go on." Jacob prompts.

"Look in the back of the seat pocket in front of you. A copy of the email is there."

Mr. Knight,

If you're reading this letter, it has gone way south. It means you don't have the code or the money and the buyer has been stolen from. The buyer will not be a happy camper. The potential for domestic terrorism may be running rampant in your mind now, but it's not in mine.

David, my son, must be protected. I've sent word to Jacob. He'll come. I've also left all the information that I've gathered in a place Jacob will know. Tell him it's next to the pack of wild dogs and to remember he's the piggy, he'll know. This is not a request. I've left some items in place. If Jacob doesn't come, a newspaper will publish his fortune and son in his hometown. If you don't help him protect my son and David should disappear and or die a liberal paper will get some interesting files on the things we've done together for the good of the people over the last couple of years.

At the end of the day, you may work for the people, but I live and die for David, my greatest accomplishment.

Get going your 3-day clock starts when Peter meets Jacob. Best Simone Johns.

Jacob folds the paper and puts it back in the seat.

"Does it make sense to you?" Mr. Knight askes.

Jacob looks out the window at the passing cars.

"Hey! Does it make sense?" Mr. Knight asks again.

"The question you want to ask me is, do I know where she left things. The answer is yes." Jacob says. He sees Mr. Knight's shoulders relax.

"The other question you want to ask me is will I tell you and the answer to that is I can't."

Mr. Knight glances into the rear-view mirror and takes a turn off the road.

"Her message also says not to trust you and tell no one," Jacob says.

Mr. Knight pulls onto the local roads, and Jacob sees the sign that says: "Sanctuary in 6 miles".

"I had no doubt she would do that. We just want to know will you go get it?" Knight asks.

"Yes, I'll go, and you can follow along, as I go get whatever it is she left. All of this is done for David. Do you know if he's my son?" Jacob asks.

"I didn't need to know that information." Mr. Knight replies.

"Ah we're back at the word games" Jacob sighs.

"What do you want to know Mr. Costa?"

"Nothing, it doesn't matter. You make sure David and Isabella Nunez are safe, and I'll bring you back what she left."

"Listen, we are not a sitting service. David is a –" Knight starts.

"You make sure both are safe, or I will become a very rich man and sell everything. I wouldn't know if I was selling to the buyer or not."

"You're not interested in stopping domestic terrorism, Mr. Costa?"

"I've learned you have to do what you can when you can and the rest you just accept. I'm sure when there's enough blood on the ground, you and your crew will be able to sort it out."

"Maybe Simone didn't know you at all?" Knight speculates.

The car pulls up to the gate. "Do we have a deal or not?" Jacob asks.

Mr. Knight rolls the window down and gives the attendant a pass. He is a young boy with long blonde hair. Jacob thought he looks like someone's son who had gotten the job by asking a favor. While the attendant went to check it on his system Knight looks in the rear-view mirror and answers.

"Your boy and the woman will be protected. Bring me back her package."

Jacob nods, and Mr. Knight drives him through the complex to a plain house at the bottom of a hill in the center of town.

"Don't forget your duty Mr. Costa and your government thanks you for your cooperation."

Just as Jacob closes the door to the car, Mr. Knight calls out.

"Can you tell me about the piggy comment?"

Jacob grins. "Simone was fond of the story of the pig and the scorpion. The scorpion rode the pigs' nose to get to the other side because he couldn't swim. The pig didn't want to trust him but figured he is safe, and the scorpion wouldn't sting him on the other side because he would be grateful he had saved his life."

Mr. Knight nods knowingly. "The Scorpion stung him on the other side."

Jacob shakes his head. "No, the scorpion stung him as they crossed the river. They both die. When the pig asked why the scorpion said it is his nature."

Mr. Knight laughs out loud. "Man, I wouldn't trade all the money in the world to be the piggy. Good day to you."

Jacob watches Mr. Knight drive away and thinks to himself. 'If I could I wouldn't be me either.'

CHAPTER ELEVEN

Friday noon, Orlando at Sanctuary

"Is she dead?" Jacob asks.

Peter smiles as he shows Jacob Costa into his office. "A body was found in the car, and the identification was made according to her dental records. There wasn't much else left."

Jacob takes a seat in the chair in front of the desk. "Ever since I've gotten here, no one seems to know how to say yes or no when I ask a question."

"Yes and no would assume that we knew what was happening or we were able to disclose the information. When it comes to you Jacob, neither one of those is true." Peter replies.

"Why did you send for me?" Jacob asks.

"It was Simone's last request."

"To tell me about my son once she was dead. Seems like she never wanted me to know about my son otherwise." Jacob suggests.

"It's true, the only way you'd ever hear about David was if there were no other options."

"And you? You're OK with this? Does David know?"

"David was raised as if I was his father."

"So, what did you tell him about me?" Jacob asks.

"We haven't said a thing. We didn't know you'd come. We'll tell David when he can handle it" Peter explains.

"And you're okay with that? "Jacob says in disbelief.

"I'm the executor of Simone's will and estate. In this situation, David being with me wouldn't be safe."

"There is a lot of concern about his safety. He's not the first boy to inherit a successful company." Jacob replies.

"He's the only living boy whose parent was involved in a deal that beyond questionable, where the money and the product disappeared on the same day. I'm sure I don't have to go into the details. Surely, Mr. Knight addressed that with you." Peter states matter of factly.

Jacob ignores the comment.

"Give the buyer, the money."

"I would, but he wants the money and the product for his trouble. If he can't have that he wants double the money. Safe Haven Inc. is successful, but we're not that successful."

Jacob sits back in his chair and folds his hands. "What makes you think I won't go tell someone. I would have thought after your conversation with Mr. Knight you'd realize there is no one to tell because we're all involved one way or another. And none of it in a good way."

"Were you watching Mr. Knight or me."

Peter stops and looks Jacob in the eye. "This is about David's safety, so I watch everyone."

"Where is David?"

Peter begins tapping his pointer finger on the desk.

"David is here. He's still facing the fact his mother is gone, and he didn't want to leave his father's side." Peter answers.

"And are you?" Jacob asks again.

"I can provide you with medical records if you need to prove your paternity."

"I'm sure you could, but I notice you're going through a lot for a boy who's not your son."

"I'm sure you know, Simone is a unique and amazing woman. I could be doing this for her and her memory." Peter replies.

"I don't want to be in this. I think everyone is lying to me or not telling me everything, and I don't like to walk blind into situations."

Peter smiles. "Simone knew you. She said you'd resist."

Jacob stands up and nods toward Peter. "Then I'm glad I wasn't a disappointment."

"Mr. Costa maybe you should look at today's paper."

Jacob turns to the couch and picks it up; the headline read "ISABELLA NUNEZ FROM RAGS TO THE SPOTLIGHT, WHO IS SHE?"

"As I said Jacob, Simone knew you. You don't have

to participate, but the people who want this money will find you and anyone that you care about to get their money back."

Jacob flips open the paper and sees a photo of him and Isabella getting off the plane.

"I wouldn't want to be you for all the money in the world right now. Caught between a dead woman and a lover." Peter says shaking his head.

"No one does things like Simone, and you are not the first person to tell me how grateful they aren't me."

"If it's any consolation, this wasn't the first time that something was leaked," Peter asks.

"What?"

"Sean Carstairs of Nova Industry decided it would be the best thing to leak that David had come into this new inheritance," Peter says through gritted teeth.

"He threw a child to the wolves?"

"You haven't met him yet but when you do keep that in mind. To Sean, we are all expendable."

Nodding towards the paper, Jacob asks. "And you and Simone were so different because – "

Peter smiles. "To Sean, we are all expendable. To Simone and me everyone is expendable for David. Have a good afternoon, with Mr. Carstairs Jacob."

CHAPTER TWELVE

Friday 12:30 p.m. Orlando on Sanctuary

Isabella is never going to be mistaken for a damsel in distress. She thought of her wide hips and said "Yup. I might be mistaken for a lot of things but not a damsel," she thought as she drove her rental truck up to the gates of Sanctuary.

"Yes miss?" the young blonde boy asks.

"I'm here to see Peter Skiseng," Isabella declares.

The young man fiddle through the pages and starts to shake his head. "I'm sorry I don't see your – "

Isabella interrupts the boy before he could finish his question. "I was supposed to arrive with Jacob Costa?"

His face goes from worried to relieved in a matter of seconds. "Ah, that's okay. He already arrived."

"Is it a security issue? You looked worried." Isabella asks.

The boy shakes his head and sighs. "Lately, everyone has been trying to see Peter. When I took this job, I thought it was going to be easy, but this is turning into a real job lately."

Isabella raises her eyebrows at his lanky body and fading tan. It must have been noticeable because the young man notices and laughs.

It was then Justice barks.

"Hey! I didn't see it. Can I touch it?" the young man asks.

Isabella is used to Justice getting attention. "Put your hand out flat first and let's see if she wants to be friends."

The young man reaches to the back of the truck. Isabella could hear Justice scrambling to her feet. Next, the sounds of the guy saying, "He licked me, he licked me!"

"He is a she. You can go ahead and pet her."

"Is she a full pit?" he asks.

"She is a purebred bull nose pit bull. Her parents were dog show winners. Justice was the runt of the litter. Now she's my baby."

Justice is standing up on her hind legs and is leaning into the young man's hand. "By the way, what's your name?" Isabella asks.

"Jeremy, Jeremy Lavell, ma'am."

"Huh, I'm a ma'am now. I don't think I'm that old Jeremy. I noticed you were kind and protective of Peter." Isabella comments.

"We all work for and live on Safe Haven. After Ms. Johns passed, everyone has been trying to see Peter. All the reporters and fortune hunter won't give him and

David any rest. We're all family here, so we want to make sure he's okay while he's grieving. My parents live on the other side of the community. The pay was good, and I didn't have to wake up too early. Besides I like David."

Isabella nods and smiles at Jeremy as he chatters on and on. "That's so considerate of you. I'm sure Peter appreciates it. The house is -?"

"Oh, it's in the middle of the town. Just follow this road, and it will take you to a cul dul sac that ends in a semi-circle next to the community center. The road is called Sanctuary Lane, and when you get to the end, the street in front of their house is called the lane. Peter lives there."

Isabella nods and then drives forward. She isn't sure how this was going to work out. In fact, more than once, she thought about turning the truck around and waiting for Jacob at the hotel. She hears the sigh of Justice and thought, maybe, Justice thought she should have stayed at the hotel as well. But Isabella couldn't imagine staying behind, while her life was being decided by others. That isn't the way she was raised, and she isn't about to let it happen now. As her father would say: "Hoy las mascaras se desprenden," Today the masks come off.

The community looks like something out of a brochure. It was perfect. The tree-lined streets, the perfect pavements. Isabella saw a couple of women out walking their small dogs. Justice took a second look at one or two of the dogs. Isabella reaches out and pats

Justice's head. She could just see the headline with that one, "Isabella Nunez's dog Justice got loose and attacked the resident dogs thinking they were toys."

"I know nothing about us fits in here. Maybe we'll be able to get in and get out." She said the words to Justice but, she knew if it involved Simone the possibility of it being easy was low to non-existent.

Simone Johns was a complicated woman. Isabella remembers meeting Simone from a party she accompanied Jacob too. Jacob had told her about Simone, but she had been nothing but pleasant. Isabella thought maybe Jacob had just exaggerated. Then Simone showed up in the bathroom and essentially cornered her.

"You're Jacob's new love/," Simone asked. At the time Isabella didn't want to cause Jacob a scene. "We're seeing each other, I think anything else is too soon" Simone replied by saying "Well, I hope you like doing things the rough, long way," Isabella remembered the first time they had met, and it had set the tone. For all the rest of their interactions.

When she pulls up on the street, a little golf cart has stopped as well. Inside was a tall, lanky man in maintenance clothes. He has one foot out of the golf cart. Isabella doesn't give him another glance because she sees the little boy in the driveway.

When she cuts the engine, the maintenance man gets back in his cart and drives away giving her a wave. She guesses he must be like Jeremy, one of the staff who cares about David. The man's leaving gives her a moment to look at the boy in the driveway.

So, this was Jacob's son. She isn't sure she could see any "Jacob" in him, but he is a cute kid.

Isabella gets out of the car. When she closes the door, the boy looks at her and stops looking at the retreating maintenance man. 'It must have been one of his friends,' she thinks. When he turns his full gaze upon her, Isabella corrects her first thought. She could see Jacob in this boy. It was the way he held his head and the light of curiosity that lit up his face.

"Hello, I'm -"

"You're Isabella Noon-ness." David completes for her.

Isabella smiles. "Have we met before?" she asked.

"No, but mommy said you would come. She told me you wouldn't be a stranger, so I could talk to you." David replies.

"I've got a dog with me, are you scared of dogs?"

"Will it bite me?" he asked.

Isabella never gets tired of that question. Had it been any other person, she would have said: "Yes, she has teeth, of course, she'll bite." But if she could be patient with Jeremy, she could be extra patient with David.

"Her name is Justice, and no she doesn't usually bite people."

The boy stood up with a stuffed toy in his arm and then walked over to Isabella.

"Can you let me see it first before it comes out?"

Cautious and smart, this boy was going to be a heartbreaker Isabella thought. "Yes, I can. "

Isabella lifts the boy and shows him Justice in the back

seat. The sturdy pit placed her rectangular head out the window. When David offered his hand palm up, Justice sniffs it and then licks him.

"Eewws" David squeals and pulls back his hand.

Isabella puts the boy down and opens the door for Justice. Justice comes out and introduces herself to David by giving him kisses while he laughs.

They walk to the driveway and Isabella looks at how deserted it is.

"David are you out here with anyone?'

"No."

"Did you tell your father you were out here?"

"No."

Isabella wasn't known for her tact. "It doesn't seem safe for you to be out here alone."

"I have Ms. Owl." He said squeezing the toy with one hand while petting Justice with the other.

"ah huh. Well, I don't know what Ms. Owl can or can't do, but I think we need to go in". She hoped Jacob was in there tearing into this Peter guy. Who would leave a child alone? Sure, everyone knows him, but it only takes one crazy to get through.

"Oh-kay. Mommy said I should listen to you."

Isabella stops. "When did you last talk to your mother?"

David looks at Isabella, and his little face scrunches up as if he was concentrating really hard. "Mommy told me you would come. She told me she would go away for a little while." Isabella was out of her depth. David is having problems with his mother dying. She can't imagine a thing. Isabella's mother was the center of the house and in most cases the hand of God.

"How old are you David/."

"I'm 8."

"Your mommy told you a lot for a little boy."

David starts to laugh. Isabella was confused.

"Mommy said little boys have big brains and I'm really smart."

"Really?'

David shook his head. "Yes, Mommy says I'm really smart, and I'll be smarter than her when I grow up."

Isabella looks at the stuffed toy. It was a bit ratty, and the eyes looked worn. It must be his favorite toy because it shows signs of constant loving.

"Did you want to be my friend," David asks

"Justice likes you, so yeah I want to be friends." Isabella agrees.

"Okay. I don't have a lot of friends, but Ms. Owl says friends can go to my room, do you want to see my room?"

"Yes, I would," Isabella says with a smile. "Do you mind if we bring Justice?" Isabella asks.

"She can come. I have toys for her."

Isabella taps David on the shoulder as he walks away. "You have a dog?"

"No, I don't, but we got some. Mommy says to be prepared."

"It seems your mom was very smart."

David smiles and tugs on Isabella's hand. "She told me stories to help me. Do you like stories?"

"I do."

David keeps chattering away. "Good, I can tell you a story while we go to my room."

Isabella nods. "Okay."

David led the way as the three of them went into the house. "So, my favorite story is about a pig, a scorpion, and a lake – "

CHAPTER THIRTEEN

Friday 12:30 p.m., Orlando on Sanctuary

Things are no longer simple.

John looks at the woman who had driven up in the truck as he rode by in his golf cart. She has a dog. John hated dogs.

"Why were things getting so complicated?" John mutters to himself.

John didn't understand why things aren't going like they were supposed to. First, Carstairs lost his money, 85 million dollars and failed to give him his software, Houdini. Jane didn't know where the money or the software was. John had to assume she didn't know anything to tell, for now. He reached out to his other sources. His network is more reliable than Carstairs. He has people already on Sanctuary when they discovered what Simone Johns was working on. He felt pretty confident that if the product or his money had hit the open market, he would know about it. Jane thinks he is a weak link. Normally, John wouldn't mind, and he'd take his time to get what he wanted from Jane but, John felt like he'd been in one place for long enough.

John went back to his house. When John walked into the house, the doorway opens up to the living room. He purchased some furniture from the Salvation Army in the area. He had to pay a fee to have them deliver it but, he was okay with that.

He checks his phone and looks on the groundskeeper; there are no maintenance tickets that needed to be addressed. So, he turns on the television. The news is still reporting about Simone's death.

The newscast starts with a picture of Simone Johns on the screen.

"Today, we say goodbye to one of our own. Simone Johns, 43-year old owner of the educational software company, Safe Haven. Best known for her educational game line called 'I can do it too.' A line of games that simulates the work day of members in the I.T field. It was heralded as an early learning tool to introduce science and technology to children and a bonding tool for busy parents in the I.T. field to share experiences through gameplay. She was also heralded as a role model for what other African American girls can do in the technology field; She will be missed."

'She should have left her affairs in order John thought. I'm missing her, my money certainly missed her, and my product hopefully didn't stay with her.' John shakes his head.

He thought back to the woman who arrived in the truck. She is cute. She isn't a small woman but one of those real woman who ate food and had love handles. John smiles. He is a simple man with simple tastes. The dog would have to go. Then, he'd see what kind of woman she is. He would teach her good from bad. She'd fight for what he believed in. She might be the kind of the woman he was looking for. Finding a simple woman to go in his life would help him live quietly.

He just hoped she doesn't get in his way.

CHAPTER FOURTEEN

Friday 2 p.m. Orlando at Nova Industry.

Jacob waits until the boardroom has emptied out so there would be no witnesses. Jacob clears his voice to get Sean's attention.

"Sean Carstairs?"

Brown eyes assess Jacob, and then he took note of their lack of audience.

"I'm Sean Carstairs, Mr. Costa. I'm the owner of – "

"You're the one who leaked the information about David being the heir to a million-dollar company and Simone's death."

"Mr. Costa, I know it seems extreme – "Sean begins as he shrugs his shoulders.

"Extreme? You're the man who would sell a child's life for the hope of information on an illegal deal?" Jacob asks incredulously.

Sean's eyes narrow and he takes a seat. "I can see you don't understand. I'm sure when Peter told you this information it was in the worst light."

"It's hard to put selling a child in a good light."

"Who do you think you are to come here and cast judgment as if you're so pure? None of you may believe me, but I did this for David! If I hadn't put the word out about him now, Peter would have hidden him. He would have doomed that child to a life of running and living in shadows."

"So, you did it all for David?" Jacob asks sarcastically.

Sean sat at the board table. He spread his hands out. "I didn't say I was a boy scout Mr. Costa but, I'm a businessman. "

"In this case, the fate of a boy and a business issue has to be resolved quickly." Jacob sat on the other side of the table. "I don't trust you, but I will listen to you for a moment. So please go ahead and tell me how you were killing two birds with one stone for David's sake of course."

Sean sighs. "I knew Simone. I knew David was her world. I'm not going to say that I wasn't interested in finding the buyer. I was, and I am. I made what I thought was to be the right decision at the time. I looked at all of my options and did what I thought would help both parties."

"The problem Carstairs is that after you looked at all the options, you thought putting an 8-year-old on a hit list was an option. A man who will sell innocence can't be trusted. You could have said you were the heir apparent."

Sean sneers. "And you're so much better?" "I think

it's convenient for you to show up now. Simone is dead, and now David's father shows up. I'm not sure how you all do it in New York, but fathers claim their children before they become multi-millionaires."

"If we follow your logic, I should have assessed the situation and showed up saying I was the heir apparent and liquidated the company."

"I didn't say that."

Jacob sits back in the chair and folds his hands on the table. "I'm not here to criticize or to pass judgment. I'm here for us to come to an understanding of how things will be going forward."

Sean says wearily." Look, I didn't know you before today. The rumor is Simone stole the money and the merchandise. She may have hidden it before she was killed. If you know where either one of those items are we can go get them, and everyone can go home."

Jacob shakes his head. "I don't know anything. Until it's in my hand, what I have is all speculation. I can forget a lot of things, but one of the things I noticed you didn't bring up is you are listed as the seller of the merchandise. You say you care for David's welfare, but I don't agree with your methods. What I think we have to do is to agree to share what we have with one another and to work with each other to get out of this mess as soon as possible."

Sean nods his head in agreement. "I own the company called Nova Inc. We have dealings in and out of the web. If there is a lead, we can start I can help you. And yes, Nova and Safe haven are listed as the sellers. So, I have a vested interest. That doesn't make me evil Jacob, just a little more focused on the end goal."

"Right now, we all know the same thing, and we all have the same goal. The goal is to keep David safe first and then to deal with the missing money and code."

"Of course," Sean says as he nods to Jacob.

"If I need something I'll make sure to call you."

Jacob stood said his pleasantries and then left. A few moments later Jane Smith walked in.

"You follow him and make sure you report every day. Simone was right he is one of those Good guys. He's not telling me everything, and I need to know."

"He spoke with Mr. Knight."

Sean shakes his head. "Why do people make things so complicated? Bring in Mr. Knight if you find him. I think we need to make sure we're all sharing. And just for precaution sake, reach out to your contact on Sanctuary, let's see if we can have David visit with us for a bit."

CHAPTER FIFTEEN

The Birth of a cover – about eight years ago
"You want to have the epic fight all of the time. I don't
want to fight all the time. When I come home I don't want to
fight with the person I'm going to bed with."
Jake yells the words, and they pierce Simone's heart.
"I need your support now Jake. I have an opportunity to
open a company, and I want to do it right, and I want to do it
with you."
"Cece, I'll support you no matter what, but I won't walk
away from my career to do it."
Simone's frustrations are clouding her thoughts. She can
feel the anger, and still, she can't clear it away. They are
living in a condominium on the east side of Manhattan. The
condo is on the 14th floor. The bedroom transitions from red
cherry blossoms to a floral print on the walls and into the
living room. They make good money, but with Sean's offer,
she could do so much more. After the company is situated, she
could help Jake. Most important she would be able to keep

secrets from Jake.

'Why was Jake so stubborn,' Simone thinks.

The condo walls are closing in on her, and for once she has a chance for a solid opportunity.

"We could do more. I want to open a company." Simone says firmly.

"Cece, I want you to open the company but, I won't walk away from what I've got to work for you. If you want the opportunity, go. We can travel for a little while and see how it works."

"You'd rather be separate from me than to work for me?" Simone says in a hurt voice.

"CeCe, I'm not saying that. I'm saying that I've just started my career and moving to another state, I'd have to start over again."

"Jake how can you even compare your job to me getting the opportunity to run my own company! Your job can be anywhere. Any idiot could see a company would be more profitable to us. Don't let your ego get in the way or a real opportunity!"

Jake stops. "Cece, why are you pushing this? We agreed. We'd both have our careers. I told you I'd take care of you and stand by you if that's what you wanted."

"But the rules don't apply if I can take care of you?"

"Cece, it wouldn't matter if you had all the money in the world. I'm a man. I won't let a woman take care of me. If you think this is my ego, then think what you want."

Simone wraps her arms around his neck. Her hands trail down his shoulders and rest on his chest. "Is this about how I see you. I've never doubted you could take care of me. You'd always be my man, Jake."

Jake doesn't move. For the first time, Simone is getting a tendril of concern.

"Is it so wrong for me to want to take care of you?" Simone leans in to kiss Jake, and he pulls her arms away from him and takes a step back.

"Cece, I've never said no to you. When we first got married two years ago, you wanted a huge wedding. I gave it."

"It was my big day. Didn't you like the ceremony?"

"I cared about you Cece, the ceremony was for you. It was costly, and I didn't finish paying for it until a year later. You wanted to move into the city, we moved."

"We work in the city, Jake."

"The city isn't for me. I like the boroughs, Cece. Where I work and where I play are not the same."

"You wanted to go on this fast track for cash, and you've worked yourself so much you had to go to the hospital for exhaustion."

"Don't dance around it, Jake. That's not like you. You really want to say you think my working caused my miscarriage!"

Jake takes a deep breath and continues. "Everything you've asked I've given it but this one I won't do. There are some things I need in my life too. I need my job. I need to know I do something well and I need to know I can take care of myself and I'm not riding the coattails of my wife."

Simone pushes away noticing the rivulets of tears streaming down her face. "I love you Jake, doesn't that count for something? You know how hard it is for a woman in I.T. This is a chance for me to get ahead. You're a man Jake. Let's *face it you can move anywhere and make a career."*

"I care about you Cece but, a relationship is about give and take. The only thing you've done is take. You need to make a decision. Do you want to be in a relationship where we both get a say, or do you want a puppy to follow you around?"
Jake picks up his jacket and walks out of the condo.

Simone falls to the floor. She waits for Jake to come back. She thinks he will say he is sorry and that he misunderstood. Hours went by, and he doesn't return. When daylight turns to night, she gets up from the floor. She packs her belongings and then makes a call.

"Mr. Carstairs, I'm ready to go."

"I'm glad to hear it. How much time will you need to wrap things up?" Sean asks on the line.

"I won't need time to move. I can leave tonight." Simone replies.

CHAPTER SIXTEEN

Friday12:30 p.m, Orlando on Sanctuary

Peter has Isabella in his sights as soon as she steps out
of the truck.

He had anticipated her to come with Jacob earlier.
After the conversation and her lack of appearance, he
knows Jacob's relationship is having some difficulty
with the surprise Simone left them. He wishes he could
help them, but in the grand scheme of things, this
wasn't his concern. When the dog came out, he was a
little nervous, but when he saw her introduce the dog to
David, he knew everything he needed about Isabella. It
is a shame; Isabella seems like a nice woman.

Peter trusts animal instincts, and if that powerful dog
is willing to follow her commands off the leash and roll
over for David, then he will give her the benefit of the
doubt.

He waits for them to come in the house. He hears
David getting ready to tell his favorite story. He smiles.

Count on Simone to teach her son stories that were darwinistically practical. He clears his voice, and Isabella's smile falls away, and she looks at the man.

Justice walks to Peter and sniffs him. After that, she returns to Isabella's side.

"Daddy meet Justice. She's really sweet. Justice likes Ms. Owl." David says practically jumping with every syllable.

"I heard you, David." Peter acknowledges patiently.

"Daddy, I was thinking..." David says as Peter picks him up in his arms.

"I'm sure you were, you a little monster but, we can talk about your thoughts later okay? I want to meet your new friend." Peter replies.

David shakes his head and looks at Peter confused. "She can't be a new friend. Mommy said she was coming."

Peter's smile falters for a moment and then returns. He taps David on his nose. "You're right. I must have forgotten. Why don't you go play for a bit, so I can talk with her?"

"Okay, but don't keep Justice too long." David whines.

Isabella laughs. "David, did you want to play with Justice?'

Peter clears his voice. "Is it safe? I know she's okay now, but I've heard so much about the breed that -"

"Justice is safe. I take her around other children and dogs all the time. We take her to adult homes. We were hoping to get her certified as a service dog. "Isabella brags.

Peter called Justice. "Justice?"

The dog walks over to Peter and looks over its shoulder at Isabella.

"Make friends Justice" Isabella commands.

Justice rolls on her back and turns her head towards Peter with her tongue hanging out the side. Peter laughs. "Okay. David, you and Justice can play for a little bit."

When David leaves with Justice Peter shows Isabella into his office.

"I'm glad to meet you, Isabella Nunez." He says motioning her to a seat.

"I'm sorry I don't really know you."

"I'm Peter Skiseng"

"No, no. What I mean is, of course, I know your name as I came to the house. But I don't know what your role is in this whole affair." Isabella presses.

"I'm the lawyer of -'

Isabella held up her hand and shakes her head. "No, I mean who are you. Are you Simone's lover? David's father? You know who you are? The important stuff."

Peter smiles. "I want you to know I read a full security dossier on you and it didn't' do you justice."

"What did it say?" she asked curiously. "I don't think anyone has ever thought I was that important to investigate me. Most of the times people ask me, and I tell them."

"It said you were Isabella Nunez, the ninth child of Imelda Nunez. Your last name is the same as your mother's because your paternity was unknown. It seems the paternity of all of your siblings were unknown. All in all, Imelda was a hard-working woman. Each one of her children went on to become successful in their own right. You all send money to her every month, and she never has to work another day in her life. She works as a home health aide because she believes in helping others.

It appears you and your siblings took on her work ethic and you've made a name for yourself as being a fixer. People come to you when they can't figure out their problems. When companies have a leak in their data centers, they call you. Your services are highly sought after, and you charge a handsome fee for those services. Recently, you decided to merge your business with Jacob Costa. His company specializes in penetration testing. The two of you together have made a name for yourself. All of that tells me nothing of the woman before me."

Isabella smiles. "Not bad but don't start with the foolishness. You didn't do this in the last couple of days. I can't even verify all of my siblings, and I know where they are. You've been planning this for a while."

Peter smiles. "See the data couldn't tell me that about you."

"There's nothing to say. I'm a simple Latin woman. I love hard. I work hard, and I'm faithful to the family. Right now, I feel like you're threatening my family. I want what's best for Jacob."

"We are in the same place then Isabella. I'm doing

what I have to do for my family too." Peter says solemnly.

"Then tell me about you so I can understand why we're here." Isabella prompts.

"I started out with a good family. My family is in politics. There weren't in anything big, but they were hoping. They had sons who were Harvard graduates. We participated in all of the African American cliques. We knew the right people, and we mingled with the right families. I have an older brother who was ready to make a run for a representative seat. I had graduated from Harvard Law and was working at a law firm as a clerk with potential." Peter laughs.

"Funny, when I started working as an admin assistant and the guys I use to order lunch for had an internal bet on whether I could learn to code. I'll have to remember when I tell the story that I say that I was an Admin with potential." Isabella said.

"I'm impressed, Ms. Nunez. I bet those guys were surprised."

"My mother had a saying "Don't spit in the air because it might land in your hair. The guys didn't have that wisdom. As for my father, I knew him. He didn't live long, but I knew him for five years."

"I'll note that. As to my tale, to be short, my brother ran for representative on being honest. When the firm I was working at came under suspicion, this was the first test for him in the public eye. My family gave me a talk about going through the motions, and so he had me arrested. I thought it would be a preliminary trial and it would be thrown out. My brother decided I needed to be convicted to prove to others that he wouldn't play favorites."

Isabella gasps.

Peter laughs. "The true shame here is he didn't get the office. I, on the other hand, wound up with a five-year sentence and a date to review my license afterward. I think we all thought the license review was for the papers. I had resigned myself to never practicing law and not mixing with my family. Skiskeng's don't affiliate with convicts. Simone ran a program in the prison. She had a training class. I had been in there for a year. I had established myself as nonviolent, and they let me takes classes. The wardens realized I had a brain and I became a modern-day Joseph We met, we talked for six months, and then I was out three months later."

"That must have been some kind of romance. "

"I think you understand being with a person who is committed to a cause and focused." Peter offers.

Isabella grins. "Yeah, it's totally hot!"

Peter laughs. "I'm glad I talked with you. I thought… I thought you were going to be much worse and you would have been entitled. But it would have made an already bad situation tenser."

"I wanted to be a pain, but I gave it some thought and knew it would hurt Jacob and Jacob is always my first concern."

"Simone is mine."

"And David?" Isabella asks.

"I think David is everyone's priority."

"What a lawyer answer. "Isabella jokes.
"Occupational hazard."
David calls out. "I think we're hungry."
"Let's go feed the kids," Peter says.
"I'm liking you better already."

CHAPTER SEVENTEEN

Saturday 9:00 a.m. Orlando on Sanctuary

Sleeping in your fiancée's ex-wife house is an endless night of tossing. It was like sleeping at your parent's house with your husband. You knew you we old enough to do whatever you want to in the bed, but you feel like they would hear or somehow, they would know one or both of you are thinking about sex.

Isabella woke up cranky. They only happy people in the house is David and Peter. David and Justice were getting along as if they were long lost, friends. When Isabella sees Peter, he gives her a small smile. She doesn't return the smile. It is morning, and she hasn't had coffee.

David has gone to play outside in the driveway, leaving Isabella, Jacob, and Peter alone at the kitchen table. There are no morning salutations. Peter sits down and starts talking to Jacob.

"What have you decided about when to tell David?"

Peter asks.

"I've decided not to tell him anything right now," Jacob replies.

Bella puts her coffee cup down and looks at them both.

"What is this some man thing that I don't get?" Isabella asks. "We come all this way because she says he's your son. We have all sorts of bad people looking for us, and then you both have some male psychic moment. Because that is the only reason, I can understand why we're not telling David and how the both of you have agreed on this." Bella says exasperatedly.

Peter smiles at Bella and then turned to Jacob.

"You must at the very least lead an interesting life. She doesn't hold her opinion about anything does she?"

Jacob laughs and looks at Bella. "No. A lot of things may be said about Bella but keeping her opinions to herself definitely isn't be one of them."

Bella rolls her eyes and pats Justice who lays at her side. Then Bella looks out the window and sees David in the driveway.

"David is outside." Isabella states.

Peter turns and sees David hugging Ms. Owl.

"Yes, sometimes he goes out and plays for an hour to get sun. He'll only be an hour, and then he comes back in." Peter explains.

"How did the meeting with Carstairs go?" Isabella asks. Jacob stops and gives her a look. Isabella throws her hands up exasperated.

"So, what? You two can discuss if we are going to tell David about his dad but when it comes to talking with Sean that was a secret. I give up. Pass me some more coffee." Isabella declares.

Jacob laughs under his breath. "I wouldn't trust him as far as I could trust him. He's the type of person that sacrifices everyone to get what he wants." Jacob replies.

"Simone usually meets him off the grounds. He's one of the few exceptions about how to handle Safe Haven business", Peter explains.

"I'm going to leave to see if Simone left anything. It'll take me two days, and then this will be done. I think we need to have a plan in case there's nothing there. Or the other possibility that's its already been stolen before I get there." Jacob ventures.

Isabella looked at Peter and said, "I noticed you didn't ask him where he was going?". Justice picked up her head at the same time, and her ears went up. Isabella patted Justice's head. "See even Justice was a little shocked and wanted to hear this answer." Bella teases.

Peter finishes taking a sip of his coffee and replies. "It's not my business. Simone and I believed that everyone had a role and we all had to stay in our lanes."

Justice got up on all fours and Jacob called her.

"Jus' what's wrong?" Isabella asked as Justice rose.

Bella looked up and saw a man approaching David. He was waving David to him, and David looked unsure but took a step towards the stranger.

Isabella patted Justice on the side and spoke. "Jus' go get David."

Justice ran out of the kitchen and to the open door.
When they all stood up the man-made eye contact with
Isabella. In moments Justice was running towards
David, and the man ran off into the rows of houses.
Everyone ran towards David then. Peter got there first
and grabbed David up in his arms.

He held David close.

"David, you were talking to a stranger." Peter
murmurs in David's hair.

David pushes away from Peter's chest and looks at
him confused. "He said he wasn't a stranger and that
mommy sent him. He said mommy was waiting for
me."

Peter held David close and the closes his eyes.

"What did I tell you about mommy?"

David wiggles down and looks at everyone standing
around. He hid his face in Ms. Owl.

"You told me that mommy was sleeping and that she
wasn't coming home for a while. But – "David begins
but clamps his mouth shut at the last minute.

"But what David?" Isabella asks as she moves closer
to David. She runs her hand through his thick mop of
hair.

"Ms. Owl says mommy is coming back and I just need
to be good and wait." David murmurs.

Peter swears.

"Well, maybe Ms. Owl is right. But I think that if your
mommy is coming back, she'll let Ja- your daddy know,
right?"

David nods his head.

Peter looks over David's head and pulls his phone out of his back pocket before walking back to the house.

"Jeremy, did you let anyone on the property this morning?" Peter askes on the phone.

"No, no Mr. Skiseng. All's quiet" the boy replies.

Peter walks David into the house.

Bella grabs Jacob's arm. "This is getting out of hand. I think you should leave this afternoon to get what you can. If they are desperate enough to try to make a play for him in daylight. Things are changing faster than we thought."

Jacob nods.

As Bella watches Jacob get ready to leave and Peter enters the house with David in his arms, Justice nudges her hand. Bella bends down, pats Justice and gives her kisses.

"You did good today Jus'. It looks like it was a good idea that we did come along." Isabella praises Justice.

CHAPTER EIGHTEEN

Rebellion
"Simone, we need to talk," Sean says as he walks into her office.
"Sean, I'm busy. Can we schedule this for -"?
"No, we can't." He says as he cut her off. "You canceled the contract with the Synergy company."
Simone prepared herself she knew this confrontation was coming eventually.
"Yes, Sean I did. The issue is they are just a front for the Russian government," she explains.
"Lots of companies are fronts for other countries Simone," Sean replies.
"That's true, but this company has gone to every other American boutique. With a track record like that, it makes me think they want to get in bed with an American company for all of the wrong reasons."
Sean paces the room in front of her office. "What were you thinking! The money was good, and I know you could do it. If

we did this, it would be the beginning of a very lucrative relationship."

"Did you hear what I just said?"

"I did, you think Synergy may have some negative opinions about the United States. We can watch them. The money is impressive." Sean says through clenched teeth.

"It's not about the money Sean. I research every person we are going to deal with. This company you wanted to work with wasn't a company that I felt comfortable with. We can always make money, and we don't need to accept everyone. We don't want the reputation that we'll take any contract." Simone counters.

"I -I can't believe we are having this conversation again. This is technology. You don't know how long you will be able to keep up. The web only rewards those who can do miracles on demand. This company is big, and they will spread our reputation, so we can get in a position to control the market. Besides, when did you start thinking about what the company's reputation should be. You run Safe haven, and I run Nova."

"Nova and Safe Haven are tied together when it comes to reputation. I need to be careful. "Simone said what she thought was obvious.

Sean looks at her and starts to laugh. "Do you think you get to run things the way you want to? I run this. You are just a figurehead at best. You've got skill, but I'm still in control, Simone."

Simone stands up and closes her eyes before she takes a breath to say what she needs to say.

"The company has dealings that might hurt the United

States," Simone says calmly.

"The United States doesn't exist on the web. Money exists and -" Sean continues.

"And I won't let my company do anything to hurt the country I live in. I won't be a knowing and willing partner to make something that will hurt others." Simone states.

Sean stops and starts to laugh again.

"I don't think I can say it any clearer but let me try. This company. You don't have a company. You are here because I gave this to you. You need to remember your place and do what I tell you or I'll take it back and leave you where you were. A lone female who had to result to hanging out in a van to keep her position." Sean sneers.

"I don't deny you helped me get here, but I've been the one to keep both companies at the top of the pack. When code is wanted on the web, they come to you for a meeting, but they come to me when they want product. Safe Haven has moved to the top of the educational market, and we are now a standard in schools, and we are expanding every day. So, I won't take away what you did for me but don't' take away what I did either."

"You've forgotten your place, Simone. I see giving you a little rope has made you think you are in charge. Run the company little girl. Play with the big boys for now. When the time is right, you'll remember I'm the one who put you here. You're here because I say so."

With that Sean walks out of the office. A few moments later Peter walks in.

"I could hear him down the hall."

"Peter, he isn't going to go away," Simone says concerned.

Peter walks to Simone and pulls her into his arms.
"We'll handle it."
"What about David?"
"David is first, but we have to prepare, just in case," Peter
warns.

CHAPTER NINETEEN

Saturday 1:00 p.m. Orlando on Sanctuary

"What are you doing?" Bella almost dropped her phone when David spoke. David was dressed in a Superman outfit. Blue pants and, a shirt with an 'S' on it and a cape. He with his faithful Ms. Owl with him gripped in his arm. She didn't hear him enter the bedroom. The room wasn't large. It had only a bed and a desk in it. It is probably a guest room which is just fine with Bella. She had returned to the house after Jacob said he was going to see Sean after a phone call. They had shared terse words.

"You don't think it's a little odd that Sean wants to see you again, after what happened this morning?"

"Bella, you're right. Sean probably had something to do with this morning, but I need all of the facts before I go." Jacob explained.

"You and your need to have all of the facts. We already know Sean's a snake. Why do you need to know what kind of snake? Let's just avoid him altogether, get our information and move on." Isabella pleaded.

She hadn't relented. Jacob hadn't budged. In the end, they agreed he would go see Sean and then stay at a hotel close to the airport. He'd get the early flight and be on his way. He'd go where he needed to be and then catch a flight that night, and this would all be done by tomorrow night.

Looking at David standing in the doorway, she knew Jacob had been right. This little boy shouldn't be ripped from all that he knew. Jacob needs all the facts, and this was the only way to get them. She doesn't have to like it. Isabella can't go with him. Jacob asked her to stay and watch his son. How could she have said no to that? If she can get some intel, then she wouldn't feel so useless. That brought her to this moment and David's question.

"I was reading a text from your fa-, from Jacob." Bella had to gulp past that correction, but she did. Jacob said he would take care of telling David when he returned, and she would wait. Isabella doesn't want to be that woman who pushes things faster than what Jacob is ready for. In truth, Isabella isn't part of the psychic male trinity, so she isn't sure what they are thinking. Jacob doesn't really talk about it, so Isabella has to do what she usually does when Jacob was percolating over ideas. She waits. Besides, Isabella doesn't want to hurt David. He hasn't done anything. David is a victim in this whole affair, like her. The revelations will come in their own time.

"Did he find the treasure?"

"The treasure?"

"Ms. Owl said he's looking for the treasure, so mommy can come home."

Bella wished Jacob was here.

"Come here why don't we look at where Jacob is now." David crawls up on the bed and sits next to her.

"What are we going to do?" David asks expectantly. Bella opens her laptop and pulls him close to her side.

"So, we're going to do a couple of things. We're going to find Jacob's phone, and then his phone is going to help us."

David looks up at her and smiles. "A phone can't do that?"

"You think you know everything, little boy." Bella teases as she tickles David.

"'kay, 'kay show me," he laughs.

"Okay, young man, sit and be amazed," Bella says. David leans against Bella. She looks down at him and pauses.

'This is Jake's son,' she thinks. He looks up at her and says "You gonna show me?"

"Let's go." Bella opens her laptop and logs in.

"What's your password?" David asks.

Bella nudges David. "What do you know about passwords?"

"My mom taught me. I know all the important passwords."

"Well, I'm glad you know them, but you're not

going to know mine, and you won't need it because the only time you should be on this machine is if I'm with you."

A dejected David looks at the screen. "Kay." After a couple of keystrokes, her screen comes up.

"Your screen is black. Did you break it?" he asks. When Isabella looked at him, she could see all the skepticism on his face at what appears to be the end of the road.

"I didn't break it. Look there is a blinking light. I can write in this black box." Bella reached over and got a device from her table.

"We need to plug this in it's going to help us. So, we know the address of your dad's phone. And we are going to ask your daddy's phone to find other addresses of things that want to give him their addresses."

"Things have addresses?" David asks.

"This house has an address and machines have an address; it's called a MAC address."

"MAC for machines?"

"You can say that." Bella types in some commands and on the screen and a list of addresses show up.

"Look there they are." David squeals. His excitement is contagious.

"Wait we can do more. Now, we are going to take the addresses and put them on the website and find out what they are."

"What they are? You already said they were

houses".

"A lot of things have addresses David, not just houses," Isabella explains.

"Yes, we want to know who lives there." Bella did some more keystrokes and then found out two of the MAC addresses were cameras in the building Jacob was in. She took the MAC address and then ran a command on it.

"You are typing so fast, tell me."

"I found the address and then used a command called 'ifconfig' to get the camera to forget to look at anything. Then I'll use the camera to look through it."

"Really?"

"David, you still seem like you don't believe me?"

"Well, I only see a dark screen with lots of letters."

Bella did a couple of more keystrokes, and then the screen changed, and a screen came up showing a room full of people. David stops talking, and even Bella is amazed at the view as well.

There were several lanes with people working at a desk. The picture was only up for 30 seconds when the picture went away. On Bella's screen, she could see all of the fake MAC addresses she used to hide her trail being shut down.

She didn't know exactly what and where she had seen, but they had someone trying to hide it. She backed out and disconnected and shut down.

"What happened Isabella? The picture went

away, and you turned off your machine?" David asks.

"That's enough for today. I need to do some work, and I'll show you more later."

David didn't look happy, but he grumpily said okay. He walks to the door and turns back to a worried Bella.

"Thanks, Isabella."

The worry fell away for a moment, and she smiles back. "No problem, I'll show you other stuff later. Oh, and make sure you keep Justice with you. She was really scared this morning, that's why she came out barking."

"Great I like being with Justice too!"

David looks for Justice, and Bella picks up her phone to text Jake.

"Full house around your addy, there's a shop there, and they have a watchdog who almost got me. Be careful."

CHAPTER TWENTY

Saturday 1:00 p.m. Orlando on Nova

"Sean," Jake says, as he grips Sean's hand. "You said you wanted to see me, but I have to tell you nothing has changed since our last meet. So, I'm a little confused."

"I'm sorry for keeping you waiting. There's always someone who needs software development, and they never know how much it costs or what it takes to get it done," the well-dressed man said with a look of disgust. "I realized after you left that you were right. We should be completely open with one another. There was something else going on with Simone and me. I was on the verge of getting her to do some business with a friend of mine. I wanted you to meet him."

Jake started to speak. "I don't really think this is the right -"

Sean waved towards the doorway, and a man walked in. "I'd like you to meet an associate of mine. Roger Adams. He's with Learning time."

"Learning time? You do educational software," Jake asked as he shook hands with Roger's

Roger Adams lowered his body into a nearby seat. He was a slim man wearing an off the rack suit, cheap shoes and a ten-thousand-dollar watch. When Jake saw him, he thought Roger has just come into money or was new money. The newer the money, the flashier they were. Old money or really smart investors knew how to have hints of wealth.

"You're right. Roger is in the educational business. I wanted to put all my cards on the table, and I thought it would be good for us all to meet each other. Besides Roger wanted to meet you earlier and I hesitated."

Jacob looked at Rogers," You knew Simone?"

Rogers smiled, "You didn't know Simone. You were either with her or trying to catch up. I'm not too proud to admit. I was trying to catch up."

"The world of educational software is small. They all know you are the new owner of Safe Haven. Rogers wanted the opportunity to offer you a proposition first." Sean commented.

Jacob's phone vibrated and out of habit he looked at it and saw Bella's message. "Full house around your addy, there's a shop there, and they have a watchdog who almost got me. Be careful."

Everything had just gotten a lot more interesting.

Jacob had known Sean for less than a day. The one thing he could say about Sean was he was an opportunist. He had a set of flexible morals that would put a snake to shame. Jacob was also willing to bet this meeting hadn't come cheap to Rogers.

"Well if Sean recommends you, Of course, I'll listen to your proposition." Said Jacob.

"Thanks, Jacob, Can I call you Jake? I think we can help each other." Rogers said as he moved closer to Jacob.

"Help is a relative word, Roger. To be honest, I'm not sure I need any help at the moment," Jake said.

The elderly woman from the front peaked her head in the door and then brought in a tray of coffee and tea. She set the tray on Sean's desk and then left out.

"That woman is amazing. I can't tell you how but when we are finished with our drink she'll come in and if our drinks get cold she'll just show up. If any of my three ex-wives had exhibited that talent I'd have kept at least one," Sean said.

Roger cleared his voice and Jacob looked at the man who had a tight smile. He had reached for the tray and Jake could see he had put in three spoons of sugar in the cup of coffee so far.

"So, Roger, what's the pitch?" Jacob asked.

"It's not a pitch; it's about making a good deal. I understand Ms. Johns has left you the company and we at LT want to be there to partner with you or depending on how you feel about owning your ex-wife's company, perhaps we could even make an offer," Roger said as he leaned back in his chair.

This was the reason he did most of his work from home. Roger leaned back in his chair as if he was doing me a favor. If Jacob was honest, he would have been very open to the idea of selling the company, but he didn't want to destroy the legacy Simone had built for David.

"Let's hear your offer?" Jacob prodded.

Rogers eyes went to Sean and then came back to Jacob. Roger leaned forward and cleared his throat. "Sean said you'd want to talk about all the options first."

Jacob leaned back and looked at them both. So, it seemed like Sean had sold him on the idea that this could turn into a sale conversation. Rogers cleared his throat and started the pitch.

"As partners, we can do a join between the companies. We can provide the reach and the management to take our companies to the next level." Rogers said.

"And the brand the games will be running under will be --"Jacob asked.

"We will make a new brand to push all of our products." Roger rambled.

"Why don't we talk about the money?" Sean pushed.

. Jacob looked at them both and shook his head.

"The money is important but let's be clear about what is on the table. David's financial security and legacy. The brands under Safe Haven will stay that way. If you want to create a new game or product and you want to market that under the joint brand I'm good with that, as long as Safe Haven gets to review the product."

"Do you have a person to do the review? I know you just inherited the company we want to help you ease into this industry and find out what role you want to play." Roger held out his hand, and Sean gave him a file from his desk. He passed it to Jake. "I've included a list of people and their qualifications who would be best suited for the transitions team. Like I said we want to help you and make sure the market doesn't get antsy with the changeover. "Roger reassured.

"You've picked a team already?" Jacob said looking at both Sean and Roger. "It seems you two have been busy. I'll need to do my own research first so let me get back to you. What's your offer if I don't want to be a silent partner and let you manage? "Jacob asked.

Roger cleared his throat nervously and widened his smile. "We think you need have a chance to look at what's involved. If after that you want to review how much input, you have with the new venture we can look at where you would like to be. We want to work with you, and this is an ideal time. "

"So, why me? Did you approach Peter? Did you ever approach Simone about this? She wasn't a stupid or slow woman especially when it came to money and opportunity."

Roger's smile fell for a moment, but he quickly recovered. "Simone Johns was a strong-willed woman. It's no secret we had approached her before, but she felt as though she wasn't ready to partner with anyone. If she had, LT might have been able to assist her when this unfortunate theft happened. "

Sean snorted. "Let's be upfront, Roger. Simone's answer went more towards, she didn't need to share creative rights or a man to be successful. Roger had proposed the idea, and she shot him down saying she didn't need him. While that may have been true for her, I think you need to consider Rogers offer if only for an introductory period."

"Does that mean you're involved in the deals that need to be conducted on the dark web Roger?" Jacob asked.

Roger held up his hands. "No, but LT might have been able to get the 85 million to get the buyer off of David's neck."

"Give me a week, and I'll get back to you. As you know, there are some other more pressing items going on." Jacob said to Rogers

With a nod of agreement, Rogers stood up. "Gentlemen, I want to thank you for the time. I know I wasn't part of the original schedule, but I'm glad we spoke." Rogers shook everyone's hand and then hurried out of the office. When he was gone Jacob turned on Sean.

"What the hell was that?"

"It was money. Soon the sharks will be coming. I like Rogers. He's predictably greedy and controllable. "Sean said. "You wanted me to be open, and this is me being open."

"Sean, I have to do what Simone would have wanted. I appreciate your honesty, but I'm not ready to sell to the first friend you bring in."

Holding his hands up. "Sue me. I'm looking out for you."

"Let's put him on the side. Since I'm here I wanted to know, did she work here?" Jacob said

"She worked here sometimes. But it's the nature of the company when a high-ranking person in our field leaves we lock down the machine and wipe it." Sean said.

"You wipe out any notes that she may have on the machine? "Jacob said incredulously.

"When you've been in this business for a while. You will realize the vindictive code isn't worth the information they may have on the machine. So, yes we wipe it."

"That's a shame. Simone was a creature of habit. I figured I could look on her machine before I left. "Jacob said.

"Creature of habit?"

"She kept the same password, so I would have tried it."

"I'll bite. What does the world's meanest person have as a password." Sean asked.

Jacob smiled. "Her middle name, Evangelina. She hated it."

Sean shook his head in regret. "Her machine was wiped. It's policy protocol. All vital information is saved on network drives. No information is supposed to be kept on the local machines."

Jacob looked at Sean and thought he saw everything but the tear in his eyes.

"Look into the machine anyway she might have left something. Do you have someone who can do that?"

"I can reach out to some people," Sean said.

Sean hesitated and then looked at Jacob. "That goes both ways. You're going someplace you think she might have left something. I can reach out to some people if you don't want to go."

"I'll keep in touch. I shouldn't be gone longer than a day" Jacob said.

"I know this is important and I want to help you as much as I can. I mean the sooner this is over you can think about Rogers offer as being your partner or selling maybe. ." Sean winked at Jacob.

CHAPTER TWENTY-ONE

The Leash

They sat around the boardroom table like a pack of hungry dogs, fidgety, irritable and eager for a kill.

"Come in Ms. Johns; we've been waiting for you. There is a serious matter we'd like to discuss."

There isn't a serious matter to discuss, it was more like a serious matter I'm about to be blamed for, thought Simone.

Melvin Travane cleared his throat and opened the red folder in front of him.

What dramatic b.s., thought Simone.

"Hello, Ms. Johns, I know this meeting seems abrupt, but we were brought some information that is very concerning to us," he lifted his head and nodded at Sean Carstairs standing against the wall.

Sean was dressed in a black suit to accentuate his paleness and to be ready for Simone's corporate funeral.

"Mr. Carstairs, you are the one who recommended Ms. Johns as a potential small company to invest in?"

"I did," Sean said.

"You are also the one who has brought this evidence to the board?" he said. Sean flinched slightly. He didn't expect to get dirty he just expected the blood to fly.

"I am." He said as he looked at Simone worriedly.

"Fine Mr. Carstairs you can begin."

Again, Sean cleared his throat and looked around the room. Simone would have felt sorry for him, but she knew this was just one more way for Sean to try and control her. He had given her the cover of a toy company and had been using her skills and her company's front to work on the dark web making custom code for whoever could afford it. Simone's only requirement was they didn't make things that would America, hurting Americans was okay but not the country. Lately, Sean had said she was making a distinction without a distinction.

Gathering himself to his full height, he nodded to the speaker on the board.

"We'd like you to explain what things you have observed." Mr. Travane said.

"Well, I think it started two quarters ago when Simone's company, Safe Haven were dropping, and her primary competitor Learning Technologies had just come out with a new product."

"Quarters come and go, Mr. Carstairs. Are you saying she had never had this situation before in the last two years she's been heading the company? If so it seems you have been remiss in your duty to us."

"No, she's recovered before. I believe it was the added pressure of her newborn son that made this situation unique.

I think it was just the stress of it all."

Simone curled her hands around the armrests. He thought to use her 1.5-year-old against her. She'd taken David to work with her almost every day.

"I saw she was becoming worried and unsure of herself and I tried to offer my assistance."

Simone tapped her fingers on the armrest. I guess offering sex could be seen as some type of relief but that wasn't what she wanted from Sean, Simone thought.

"Did she take your help?"

"No, she didn't. In true fashion with her paranoia and unhappiness at the time she refused any help, even when I offered to send some trusted consultants in the business to help her. I reached out to a doctor, who suggested her mood swings could be part of post partem depression." Sean said with just enough worry in his voice.

Simone could imagine the type of help they would provide. They would help themselves to her system and try to find out where she kept all of her company's secrets, she thought.

Travane nodded. "Did she give any reason why she didn't want the help from you."

"She said she didn't need any help from any of the spies I wanted to send to her."

Well at least he got that right, thought Simon.

"Continue Mr. Carstairs"

"Then she came to me and said she had a new idea and it would be better than Learning Tech. She kept saying it would be a great discovery. I was skeptical. There hadn't been any news about development and then she had a breakthrough."

"What did you do after that?" asked Travane.

"I started my own investigation into her project. If it really was that big I wanted to get an idea of how to help. I asked her to give me the highlights, and she refused. Every time I tried to do something with her, she was defensive and angry."

"Did you think the behavior was odd?"

"I did but she's has been a great leader and an excellent programmer. To be honest, I thought it was just the stress of having a new son. I know it can be traumatic for men on my team, I imagine her being alone, and a woman the stress of running Safe haven has to be even more so. So, I waited until the last moment and then demanded to see the project. She told me to leave, and then I knew I had to be worried."

"And you knew because?"

"Suspicious behavior from a programmer usually leads to illegal collaboration or even worse I was concerned there was no project. So, I have a backdoor into her company, and I looked on her hard drive for the information. And what I found was a genius learning game. The problem was I had already seen this game."

"Explain it clearly Carstairs." Travane said.

"I'm friend with the CEO of Learning tech, and he had already demoed the game to me. I knew then why she had been so secretive. She'd stolen the game from her competitor."

Simone didn't move. She hadn't made a game. She had been doing all of Carstairs side development. She'd been so busy looking at the cash she forgot she was in bed with a snake. Although she almost laughed at the concept that he would be able to get into her machine through a back door. He was thinking highly of himself these days.

Travane looked at Simone. "Carstairs are you sure you saw

stolen game plans on Ms. Johns computer?"

Simone didn't turn when Carstairs answered, "Yes, I saw the game she stole from Learning Tech."

The boardroom was silent, and they waited. They waited for her to defend herself. They waited like sharks in bloody water. Simone turned to Carstairs.

"Well done, Sean. I'm almost jealous." Simone whispered to him alone.

"Gentlemen, it seems we have already made our decisions so what's next?"

The hush was broken as they looked at her with disgust and contempt. Then Carstairs spoke.

"Gentlemen, I know this is a grievous offense. I've already spoken to Travane regarding our next actions. Since I'm on good terms with Rogers the CEO from Learning Tech and she didn't take the game to market, we have no worries from that end. What I do think this means though is Ms. Johns has been overwhelmed and overworked with her new child. These things happen, and I want to make sure we don't unfairly punish her for pushing herself. From this day forward until we can review the situation later. I will be the acting CEO of Safe haven games. Ms. Johns will stay on as co-CEO, but all items will go through me. I think Ms. Johns prefers this arrangement to the legal options we would be forced to take."

Simone looked around the boardroom and memorized each and every one of them. Then she stood up.

"I'll be happy to accept Carstairs guidance and assistance, until the day he gives me back my company Safe haven."

She could see the looks of disappointment that she hadn't fought in the room. She saw the smirks of those who thought she had been taken down a peg. The only one in the room looked worried was Carstairs.

Simone walked over to Carstairs and hugged him. As he was in her embrace, she whispered.

"Live well today because tomorrow is promised to no one."

CHAPTER TWENTY-TWO

Saturday 1:00 p.m. Orlando on Sanctuary
Chapter Eighteen
John Kooma was looking at the hidden cameras in
Simone Johns house. In his basement, he had set up
three rows of monitors. The first row looked at the
house from the front exterior. The second row of
monitors watched the rear of the house and the third set
of monitors alternated between the rooms in the house.
He could usually leave it on her bedroom because she
kept that boy with her all the time.

Tonight, the house was full. In Simone's study was
Peter. Peter the lackey. He was looking through papers.
His type was all the same. He probably went to some
fancy school and then got a good hookup to be at the
beck and call of Ms. Johns.

John looked at guys like Peter and knew they thought
they were better than him. John smirked. Who's better
now. I'm not the one being watched like a bug under a

microscope, John thought.

The second screen was focused on David's bedroom. The room was odd the way it was shaped. John hadn't had as much time as he would've liked in that room. It didn't matter the brat wasn't in the room anyway. John panned the camera around to look for that stuffed toy, Ms. Owl. If it was in the room, it meant that David was in the bathroom. David didn't travel without Ms. Owl.

When David grew up, he'd probably be just like Peter. Another privileged kid who grew up with a spoon in his mouth. When John didn't see him there, he looked at the guest room.

Isabella Nunez was sitting on the bed. She looked like a firm woman who wasn't afraid to be herself in bed. Her hair was a mess, and she had on a loose top that was just deep enough to show she had enough chest to make it interesting. The boy David was close to Isabella. John was thinking the boy has the good taste to hang out with Isabella.

When John transferred to the camera on the other wall, he was able to view the laptop in Isabella's lap. He zoomed in and saw she was hacking. John smiled. She was decent. He was better of course. He liked her voice as well. The way her hands flew across the keyboard was sexy as get out.

John really looked at her keyboard, and then he yelled "Oh Sh-!"

He knew that room; it was Sean Carstairs coders mill. He had been interviewed in that room and had been given more than one assignment in that room. He logged on to the site and found her machine. When he got to the first MAC address, he thought he had her, but when she started to shut down, he realized that she had set up several dummy addresses. Just when he thought he had her, she turned off her machine, and he couldn't capture her address.

"Damn her!"

He pushed away from the table and went to get a beer from upstairs. He yanked the door open and then went to his living room to make a call to a person that brought only trouble. He dialed her number and waited.

"Hello, John this isn't a good -?"

John gritted his teeth. "Listen, I just stopped Isabella Nunez from breaking into your site. It seems that you don't have the situation under control."

"John, you need -." Jane Smith said.

"Jane, I need to be seen tonight. If anyone found out how bad this is going, you'd have more than the mysterious buyer questioning Nova.

She didn't answer.

"I'm taking care of Jacob personally tonight and then I'll come see you." She said

"Come and see me now. I want to make sure we are on the same page." He said and then hung up.

Sean had lost control of the situation. That's what happens when you can't do the simple thing.

CHAPTER TWENTY-THREE

Saturday 9p.m Orlando, Sanctuary

Ms. Owl, David's stuff toy vibrated just enough to wake him from his sleep. Isabella had just laid him down for the night. She had read him a story and patted him on his back just like his mommy use to do.

"Day- vid," the mechanical voice said and then followed it up with another vibration.

"I'm up; I'm up." David moaned.

"Me face door." The voice said. With a heavy sigh, David lifted the toy, so it faced the door. He didn't have to see the face to know what was happening. The eyes would blink once, and the door would lock. After he heard the electronic click, he pulled Ms. Owl to his chest.

"Switch," the voice said.

Again, David was a little annoyed. He wanted to get into his bed and lay down. Now that Isabella and his dad were here, he felt safer. He needed them and Ms.

Owl. His mother had told him daddy would tell him
what to do, and his mother never lied to him.

"The switch, the switch," mumbled David. He threw
his legs over the side of his bed. He went to his desk and
underneath it was a button. His mom had put the
button there because his mom said sometimes people
wanted to watch him and this button would fix it, so no
one could watch him.

"All done Ms. Owl."

"Pack Go Bag"

All of the sleep fell away from him.

"What did you say?"

"Pack Go Bag" Ms. Owl couldn't speak in really long
sentences like he could. His mommy had told him to
listen to Ms. Owl. Sometimes mommy and him would
go over the really important things that Ms. Owl had to
say.

Mommy said when Ms. Owl said 'hide' he was
supposed to go to his secret hiding place in the attic.
When Ms. Owl said to "run," it meant go to the house to
her office or go and find daddy. The one thing mommy
taught him that scared him was when Ms. Owl said,
'Pack Go Bag.' Pack Go Bag meant they were leaving the
house and daddy would take him somewhere safe.

"I have to get Isabella and – "David began.

"No, Pack Go Bag."

David wanted to listen to Ms. Owl, but Isabella was
really nice, and she couldn't be so bad daddy let her put
him to bed. Daddy wouldn't do that unless he liked
her, and the only other person David had seen daddy

like was mommy.

David thought about it and came to a decision. He would pack the go bag and then tell Isabella in the morning before he left with daddy. David felt better. He went to his bed and pushed a button that opened a drawer. Inside of the draw were pre-packed plastic bags with things mommy said he would need. He went into his closet and pulled out his book bag and put the three plastic bags in his Superman book bag. After that, he zipped the book bag and put it in the closet.

"I'm done packing. Do I have to leave now?" If Ms. Owl said yes, he'd have to tell daddy and Isabella together.

"No, dark, morning Go," the mechanical voice said.

David was relieved and got back into the bed with his toy.

"Up Switch"

Feeling a little grumpy, David got out of bed and then went to the closet again and turned the switch back on. After that, he yawned and got back into the bed. In the morning he would go. He hoped Ms. Owl changed her mind, but it wouldn't matter he'd have daddy and Isabella to stay with him, that was until mommy came back.

* * *

John sat in front of the camera watching the house again. He saw Isabella put David to sleep in his bed and then go down to talk to Peter. He watched them thinking something else might be happening, but this was going to be another dull night of surveillance. He turned the camera back to David and saw him yawning. The kid was quick. Guess he needed a bathroom break like he did. The beers were starting to pour through him. If he didn't want to miss anything, he better start drinking some coffee. The boring surveillance made him anxious to see Ms. Jane. He was a simple man, and all he asked was that people comply with his simple commands.

CHAPTER TWENTY-FOUR

Saturday 9 p.m. Orlando on Sanctuary

When two I.T. people surrounded by tech couldn't contact one another, one of them was either in trouble or dead. Those were the thoughts that ran through Bella's head. She had put David down to sleep hoping that Jake would reply to her text at the very least but, she'd gotten nothing. The story she read to David had never seemed so long. As she went to Peter's office on the first floor, she checked her phone again, and again there was nothing.

Peter Skiseng, another puzzle to deal with. Bella had looked him up online and some other sources that weren't readily available. According to her findings, Peter had once been a well to do lawyer so that panned out. The story he gave her earlier was true. That was a plus for him.

In the years since his conviction, Simone managed to get him paroled to her company. Peter took the bar in

Florida and was named Safe Haven's lawyer. Other lawyers talked behind his back, but they were all smiles when they needed to deal with Safe Haven. The relationship between Simone and Peter was unclear, but it was one of the many questions people had about the pair. It seemed like no one had enough guts to ask the question that everyone wanted to know.

The outlook bell rang. Peter was sitting on the couch with his laptop. When he saw her, he closed it and offered her a seat.

"Have a seat. Did David go to bed okay?" This was the man who had stayed with Simone. Peter and Jacob were entirely different men, but both had chosen Simone at one point. Where Jacob was down to earth, Peter looked like he was born in a well to do family.

"He went down without a fight. I think the day has been exhausting for him and for me. I sent Jacob some information, and I haven't been able to confirm he got it."

She sat down on the couch and faced Peter. When she looked up, she found herself the sole focus of his stare. She thought he would continue to work while she spoke. Now, that he was staring at her she could feel the leashed energy in him, radiating like ripples in a pond. At that point Isabella knew, Peter wasn't good like Jacob, but he was intense and there was something about him that made you think he'd keep you safe.

"Isabella? Can I call you Bella or is that term only reserved for your lover?" Peter asked.

She had to force herself not to look away. This man

was more dangerous than she originally thought. "My friends call Bella as well."

"It seems we are in a relationship of sorts and it would be best to get the awkwardness out of the way," Peter said.

"I didn't know there was any awkwardness. We've just met."

"Yes, we've just met, and we've both been introduced to an intimate acquaintance of our current partner," Peter said.

"So, you and Simone were – "

"There are no words for what we were, so I won't try to label it. What I'll tell you is it worked for us. You said you can't get in contact with Jacob?"

Bella tried to digest the information as quickly as she could. "I don't think we have the same priorities. Besides, I don't think I'm in your league. You move from subject to subject way faster than me." Bella said

Peter smiled, and Bella felt herself take a breath. Peter smiling was a beautiful thing; It transformed his face from born with a spoon in the mouth to carefree playboy.

"I think we have exactly the same priorities. You want to keep what you've got, and I want to keep what I've got. Neither one of us wants to compromise, and both of us need to resolve Simone's issues."

Isabella heard the words, but she knew there was something more. He was Simone's only lawyer for Safe Haven and for David's custody if need be.

"Okay, for argument's sake let's say we are working

for the same goals. Then what?"

"First it means we'll pool our resources together to get our mutual issues fixed, "Peter said as he moved closer.

"I want something," Isabella said.

The smile came back, and Peter looked at Bella. "Ah, it's so nice to know all of my predictions are coming true. Tell me, Bella, what do you want? I like to know my partner doesn't mind asking for what they want."

"I think I should be offended by that, but we'll deal with that later. I want to know if I can trust you to tell me the truth." Isabella asked.

He sat back and took a deep breath. "This is what I can give you Isabella. You can trust me to tell you when it's not the complete truth."

"What-?"

Peter held up his hand. "That's more than most get. I felt I owed you that, after looking at how you were voluntold into this situation."

"Thanks, I think, "Isabella said.

"Jacob is missing," Peter stated

"No, I said – "Simone interrupted.

"I heard you, and I'm telling you he's missing. If I had sent a message to the Simone, she would acknowledge that message. We'll start looking for him in the morning." Peter said.

"Jacob isn't Simone."

"Try to get some rest. I'm a relentless partner." Peter stood to leave when Bella spoke.

"Jake isn't like Simone," Bella stated.

Peter looked down at her on the couch and answered

the question as he walked out of the room. "Of course, he is. He's just the good side and Simone is the grey side, but they are both opposite sides of the same coin."

CHAPTER TWENTY-FIVE

From the Ashes

*Sean Carstairs opened his door and stuck his foot in to find
a red light shown on his black shoes. Sean had company in his
home, and it wasn't anyone he had invited. The house had a
security system that he had paid a hefty sum for. The red line
on his shoe just brought it to his attention that he will be
discontinuing the service.*

*Sean was aggravated with the current turn of events but
not surprised. Since he had set up his company Nova, there
had been a couple of incidents that have given him some
concern, but it went with the territory of dealing on the dark
web.*

*He tried to go over his latest deals. There was the arms deal
with a couple of third world countries. A very lucrative deal
with China coming up and a couple of domestic negotiations.
There wasn't anyone uncharacteristically unhappy. He had a
good reputation, and so far, no one felt jipped. He prayed that
this wasn't personal. Sean had no patience for some lover who*

was whining over what was.

Sean didn't keep women. It was just too much upkeep. He could never figure them out, and their loyalty was always in question. He sniffed the air as he walked further in. His living room was intact. The kitchen could be seen from the living room. He had an island in the kitchen that allowed the space to be opened up.

He continued through the kitchen and went down the hall to his sitting room, and that was where he found the intruder.

"Come in Sean," Rogers said from Sean's seat at his desk.

"That's good leather Rogers, better than the likes of you. I hope you haven't been sitting in that chair too long. The chair conforms to my body. What do you want?"

Rogers' eyes widened. If he expected Sean to be cowered by the gun, he was in for a surprise. Instead of going to the couch, Sean went to the small bar in the office.

"I think I'm good enough to sit anywhere I want with this gun." Said Rogers waving the gun.

Sean poured the glass and took a sip. "You see Rogers that's where you are wrong. Gun or no gun it doesn't change the man. You weren't good enough to be here before you got a gun and you're still not. What do you want?" Sean said annoyed.

"I want you to get that girl under control! He yelled.

"Ah, Roger you see that's your problem. You think Simone is doing something to you. We all have to take responsibility for ourselves. This isn't about Simone it's about you. You should face it. You're not good enough to play in this game."

Roger dropped the gun to his side.

"That's your answer. You've used me, and my company is

falling, and now she's my problem."

Sean threw back the rest of his drink and slammed the glass down.

"It's not about Simone. She is easy. Like all women, she's easy to manipulate and weak. If you're having a problem, you need to fix it and stop blaming it on people who couldn't possibly be a factor."

Rogers started to laugh, and Sean shook his head. "Rogers you're going crazy go home. "

"You're right Sean. I should go home. One of us is delusional about how all of this is happening. But more importantly one of us is delusional about how it will all end. I thought you had a handle on things, but I can see you've bought into your own stories. I'm going home just like you said and I'm going to do what I should have done all along.'

"That is?"

"Wait for the fallout and then pick up the pieces. My company has enough money to do that.

By the way, good luck with your it's not Simone theory. I'll remind you of it when she has everything that's yours."

"Simone is a woman Roger. She's a woman with a child. She's created her own box by breeding. But you're right you'll see. Time will tell, and you'll see, Simone is easy to handle."
Sean said as he threw back the second drink.

CHAPTER TWENTY-SIX

Saturday 9.30 p.m. Orlando, Sanctuary

It's hard to break in new employees.

When the doorbell rang, he opened the door and let Jane walk in. When she was in the living room, he punched her as she was turning around. She fell on the ground with a grunt. John saw her hair spread out on the floor like a fan.

"What?" yelled Jane as she inched across the floor.

"You should be prepared. It's the simple things you have to watch otherwise you will be caught unaware." John said. He watched Jane try to crawl on the floor and finally get herself to her feet. When she was up, she stood with her back to the wall and eyed John warily.

"That's very good. You're doing much better now." John said.

"Who are you and what do you want?" Jane asked.

"I know you think I'm going to kill you. I'm not. I really like you, Jane. I think the time you've been with me is good and has helped me to focus. I like that in employees. When employees do the right thing and go above and beyond to make me happy. I appreciate it."

"I'm going to see Jacob tonight. He's being brought to his hotel by some help, and we've wired the house, so he can see we have them under surveillance." Jane stammered.

John smiled and tapped Jane on the side of her head. "That was really smart of you. I saw you, and I said she is being wasted with Carstairs. I went in after you, and I looked at the electronic system. That was clever work."

Jane began speaking "Simone has a lockdown on the house, and I'm going to trigger it so the whole house will lock up. I don't want to use guns they are too loud, and there was no sense in me staying and babysitting them if the house can hold them."

"Simple, plan with simple explanations. I like that Jane." John said.

Jane backed up and rubbed her arms. "I'm glad I make you happy."

John nodded. "I think we need to talk about the basics. Your pay and how I work."

Jane nodded. "I'm sure whatever you think will be fine."

John cocked his head to the side and stood up. "Don't lie to me, Jane. My life is too simple for lies."

He could see her breathing coming in shorter gasps and her hands clenching on her forearms.

He shook his head and sat down. "Sorry, I don't mean to scare you. I like your work, Jane. I'll pay you well, and you'll give me all your talent. However, if you want to leave my employ, you'll be dead by nightfall. I do retire some staff and leave them living, not many, but the faithful earn it."

John turned to his kitchen. "I'm sorry I'm so rude. Did you want some drink, soda, water milk?"

"No, no thank you."

"Manners, I like that too. Go take care of Jacob and bring me back my property and my money. I believe in you."

Jane backed out of the house.

"New employees, they can be so hard but necessary to on board," John said shaking his head.

John went through the kitchen to go downstairs where he had set up his shop to watch little David.

CHAPTER TWENTY-SEVEN

Saturday 9.30 p.m. Orlando Hotel at Orlando Airport

Jacob didn't care what he ate right now.

If Sean had tried the same techniques with Simone, he could see her stonewalling him. If he really thought about Simone, she would have told them what they could do with that deal.

He wanted to go back to Isabella. They had decided after seeing Sean he would stay in the hotel tonight. He didn't want to tell Isabella where he was going.

The hotel restaurant was decorated in what they call vintage bronze work. Isabella had tried to convince him bronze was art. Jacob knew the bronze was just old metal. He shook his head people would believe anything if you wrapped it in enough fluff.

He ordered at the bar not wanting to sit at a table. He wasn't interested in the company and didn't want to deal with the overly helpful wait staff. He ate his steak and potatoes with a glass of wine. Sean's comments about not having Simone's machine bothered him. He knew Sean was a liar, Jacob just didn't know why he was lying.

Sean Carstairs was a person you just couldn't trust. Sean made looking over your shoulder a daily event. Jacob finished up his meal and thought about today's events. He didn't know how it would all work out, but as usual with anything involving Simone, it wouldn't be simple.

Jacob was curious about Roger and what his part in this was. He could see there was some history between him and Sean. Jacob couldn't assess what the nature of the relationship.

Jacob took his phone out and tried to call Isabella. He tried to think of a time he couldn't reach Isabella, and none came to mind. He knew something was wrong and he contemplated on calling the community and asking the security guard to go look in on them, but then Jacob stopped himself. Bella could handle it.

The bartender returned, and Jacob asked for the tab.

"No need Mr. Carstairs has a running tab here, and you're on it. It's all been taken care of. Here take an extra glass of wine."

Yeah, Jacob thought, Sean is on another level of planning ahead.

A woman sat next to him. When he looked at her, he could see straight down the vee of the dress. She was wearing a sapphire in her belly button. The dress was black. Jacob thought she was too pale to be wearing that dress. Jacob thought he'd been around Isabella too long when color distinction was still working. She had long shapely legs that ended in black heels. Taking his time to look at her again he hoped her face wouldn't shock him sober. The wine wasn't a necessity; she wasn't hard on the eyes. She wasn't a cover model, but she had a nice smile, and she looked old enough not to cause a problem.

"Do you know Mr. Carstairs?"

Jacob thought he should have known. "I know him, but you can go back to him and let him know I don't accept gifts like this. It's bad for my long-term health with my partner." Jacob pushed away from the bar and straightened his back.

"Some say you should mind the company you keep. It gives people opinions about you," she replied. "I can see you know Sean well. Can I have a drink at least? Mr. Carstairs have a couple of guys here watching. We don't have to leave together but at least let me sit with you."

Jacob was about to answer when the shadow of the two men fell over him. When he turned, he felt a prick on his arm?

"What?"

Jacob felt himself leaning towards her like the tower of Pisa, and he couldn't seem to clear his head.

The woman reached out and pulled him to her breast. "Really? I don't mind at all."

What was she talking about? Jacob thought.

She framed his face between her hands and kissed him.

"We are going to get real close tonight; you can call me Jane" she whispered in his ear.

After those words, the only thing Jacob could feel was the men grabbing him under his shoulders as the woman called to the bartender.

"If anyone asks we'll be busy."

The bartender smiled and nodded toward Jane.

CHAPTER TWENTY-EIGHT

Allies amongst thieves

Rogers walked in and saw Simone sitting with his wife at his dining room table.

His wife stood up and kissed him.

"Love, look Ms. Johns came by to thank you for all the help you've given her. I told her, you weren't sure she would be open to the help but, as you can see I was right. "

Rogers looked at his wife, Carly. She was an attractive woman, a great mother but she wasn't the brightest crayon in the pack. She could handle simple demands, and she'd been sitting with Simone for who knows how long.

"Simone, it's so unexpected to see you?"

Roger took a seat at the table. "Oh, good let me go get you a plate we just finished, but we can wait for you before I bring out dessert. Is that okay with you Simone?"

"Please, I can wait."

Carly went into the kitchen.

"What the hell are you doing here in my home?!" Roger

asked.

"I thought about meeting you at Sean's, but then I decided against it. I figured you and Sean needed some time alone, so you could understand your relationship."

Rogers shook his head. "You and Sean are so much alike."

"Wow, I never expected you to insult me," Simone said with a smile.

"What do you want Simone?"

"I want to help you and myself. I'm hoping after talking with Sean you'll see I'm your best bet."

Carly comes out at that moment with a plate.

"Have you two been talking shop the whole time?"

Simone smiled. "We didn't want to bore you, so we tried to get it out of the way."

Carly waved the statement away. "Cece it doesn't matter, this man always talks about business like I told you before."

Rogers stopped in mid-lift of his fork. "Like you told her before?"

Carly laughed. "You see, you're not the only one with a life outside of the home. Cece and I are sorority sisters. Different colleges and year but the same sorority. Sisters across the states. She looked me up a couple of months ago when she realized you all worked together."

Rogers dropped his fork.

Carly laughed.

Simone looked worried. "Carly, I told you I think we should have told him earlier."

Carly waved her comment away." Please, he's just shocked. It's fine, right love?"

Rogers looked at the meatloaf and mash potatoes on his

*plate. Carly reached over to Rogers." Oh, do you want
something? I forgot the sour cream. I'll be back."*

Rogers looked at Simone. *"You've known all along about
Sean?"*

*"No, that was a new development I found. What I do know
is your company inside and out. I've got more inlets into your
company and the code than there are holes in Swiss cheese."*

"So, what do you want? How much do I have to give you?"

Simone placed the napkin on the table. *"You see Rogers
that's where you are wrong. I'm not the same as Sean. I don't
want you to do anything. I just need you to stay out of my
way. Sean and I have to fix this between ourselves."*

"He doesn't even think you're a threat."

"I know."

"My company?"

*"For my sorority sister, your company is fine but let me tell
you a thing or two about my sister."*

Roger inclined his head towards Simone. *"You think you
know Carly?"*

Simone placed her fingers on his lips.

*"What I know is you should stop your infidelity otherwise
you might find I'm not the sister you should be worrying
about."*

"What – "

*"Don't. During these last months, you haven't noticed, but
your housekeeper doesn't do the laundry anymore. Carly does.
Have caution Rogers or the company you're trying to keep
away from Sean and me will go to Carly, and you'll be
working for her in every sense of the word."*

Carly opened the door and had a bottle of sauce and a small

dish of melted butter.

"Cece, you're leaving? We didn't have dessert."

"Please Carly, I'm not like you. I can't eat and not gain. I'll leave you with your husband. I know these moments are rare enough without me intruding."

Roger heard Carly take Simone to the door and they said goodbye. When she came back. Roger knew he had put his striped shirt in the laundry last week after he had left his latest mistress house.

"Carly, I wondered have you seen my striped shirt. I think I wore it last week."

"You wore it last Tuesday. Yes, it's in your closet ready for you."

Rogers nodded and continued to eat. Rogers was going to take his advice and do what he originally planned to do. He would keep his head down and wait.

CHAPTER TWENTY-NINE

Saturday 10.00 p.m. Orlando, Roger's house

Survivors don't forget the ones who rescue them.

Rogers certainly didn't. He walked into his office and sat in the chair he had sat in so many years and looked around his office. It was filled with all of his accomplishments, and fortunately, there were no hints of his near miss failures.

"Roger are you okay? We have to leave soon to go to the senator's ball." Rogers wife called.

"Of Course, Clarissa, one call."

"One call and ten minutes." She chided.

Roger remembered when he had been at this desk and life hadn't been this clear. When he wasn't sure if Clarissa would walk out on him or not. If he'd be able to stay in his kid's life or would he be a pariah.

He picked up the phone and called his savior.

"Hello?" Peter Skiseng said

"I'm calling you with an update," Roger said.

"Yes?"

"You were right. Sean came to me, and he wants the company."

"What did Jacob say?"

Roger laughed. "He didn't really say anything. He tossed Sean a bone, and now he's looking for Simone's P.C. "

"Good, we can use that. "Peter sighed.

"Is it true that he may know where Simone left everything?" Roger asked.

"I don't know what he knows, but we'll let everything run its course."

"You're going to take care of Sean? Tell me that you have a plan and he's going to be taken care of?" Roger pushed.

"Have patience Rogers; there isn't enough blood on the ground for a move to be made. It's about patience." Peter replied

"You and Simone were two peas in a pod. Everything was always a plan between the two of you. Nothing was ever simple." Roger sighed. "I'm so sorry for your loss. She was an amazing woman. And it's all the more reason we should make sure Sean gets what he deserves."

"Thank you, Rogers. Your heartfelt words will be remembered." Peter said.

"I'll let you know if anything comes up."

"Again Rogers, thank you. We both thank you." Peter said.

Rogers hung up and shook his head. "They were

always a strange pair."

CHAPTER THIRTY

Sean couldn't sleep. He woke up in the middle of the night with the thought of Simone's machine.

He walked into the building and went to the floor below his office. Earlier today his admin could tell he wasn't really listening to her. He waved her way several times in the day, and finally, she stopped coming in. She gathered her papers and left the office in a huff.

He walked down the dark hall until he was in his personal office. He could see they had set up Simone's old machine and put it next to his on the desk. Her machine was an unrepentant baby blue. Like most of her equipment as a reminder, she was having a baby. As if she were the only one to accomplish that feat in history.

Simone was like so many other women who thought they could do the same job as a man. Sean grew up in a house where his father couldn't find a job, and his mother was so well educated that she could. When he was 10, she left for another well-educated person. It didn't matter that his father was a coal miner and had given all he had. His mother was like most women, opportunist.

He booted up Simone's machine and put in the password. Like clockwork, it opened.

"She thought she was so smart. Let's see how dumb you really were Simone." Sean said with a sneer in his voice.

He looked through her machine, and it looked like it barely had anything of value on it. There were some folders in a directory called miscellaneous. He opened it, and there were files with names on it. One was David, no surprise when he opened it, it was pictures of the little boy. He opened the next file called Peter, and it had pictures of him as well. There was another file with his name on it.

"Any pictures of me Simone?"

He opened the file, and the screen went dark, then it opened up a command line on the screen. The title said, Houdini.

"No way, you left the code, and I was looking for it all this time?'

Sean watched as the numbers turned into Ip addresses and then established a link. In the next moment, he saw his screen with his screen name and a prompt for his password.

"Did you hide it on my machine?"

Sean went ahead and put in his password. The screen went totally dark, and then a picture came up. It was

Simone sitting in her office.

"Hi, Sean," Simone said

When he saw it, he knew it was a trap. He reached for the power button.

"Wait, I know what you're thinking I should turn this off but if you do the program will go to the end, and you will be very broke."

Sean stopped.

"So, I left this gift for you, to hurt you in the only way that matters to you. Your accounts which I am accessing right now. I mean like all of them, even the ones I'm not supposed to know about. Thanks for logging into your machine with your password it helps to authenticate on other systems."

Sean began to hit all of the buttons on the machine and then Simone morphed into a pair of oval eyes looking back at him. The eyes extended across the screen and he heard that laugh. Her face was concealed behind a veil, but Sean knew that laugh.

"Simone, even from the grave." He ranted

The veil fell away from her face, and a skeleton's face was revealed.

'Guess what you've been pwned. If you close and unplug your machine, I'll dig in, and you will never find me. If you leave it on, I'll eat away at everything on this machine and publish it on the web as well as eat away at your accounts and donate money to all of the charities you hate.

Hope you have a wonderful day!'

Sean slammed his fist on his desk.

"Simone!"

Next, Sean heard the machine, "Congratulations Mr. Carstairs, you've just donated 200,000 to the united way. Thank you for your pledge."

Sean put his machine in sleep mode and dialed up Rogers.

"Hello?" Rogers said cautiously.

"It's Carstairs, I've got a Johns virus. Do you want me to send it to you or will you come here?" Sean demanded

"A Johns virus? I can't help you. You do remember she was the one who initially wrecked my company." Rogers laughed.

"Rogers, I need this fixed. Quickly.! Sean snapped.

"There is one who could. He's called the Spider. I can put a request for him, but he chooses what he wants to take." Roger told him.

"Tell him its name his price. But do it quickly."

"I'll do my best but Sean you should understand he's selective."

"Then throw out as much money as you think it would take, but I need him A.S.A.P"

In the background, Sean heard a ping and the machine talk. "Thank you, Mr. Carstairs, for donating 35,000 to ASPCA."

"I don't care what the tag is just find him and tell him I need him to get into the machine from wherever he is. There might be a failsafe if I remove the machine."

"I'll get back to you when I have something." Roger sighed in the background the computer rang again.

"Thank you, Mr. Carstairs, for donating to -"

CHAPTER THIRTY-ONE

Night without end

Sean Carstairs had a gift and a curse, and it was standing in front of him, Simone Johns.

"Do you want to tell me about the rollout schedule for our projects?" Sean asked through clenched teeth.

"I'm sorry I don't really know the schedule off of the top of my head. I'm trying to manage my stress with the new addition in my life. I'm thinking you might be right and what I need is some time. Time to think about what I've been doing."

He heard his words coming back to him, and it took all he had not to jump across his desk and strangle her just one good time. Here she was in office, dressed in one of the long flowy dresses that went past the knee but hugged every curve along the way. All held up by those skinny straps. If she were anyone but Simone Johns he'd be looking for a way to sleep with her.

"Simone stop the crap! What is wrong with your

148

programmers? "

"They aren't my programmers. You are the CEO; they are yours. I'm co-CEO ing while I raise my child. You know what that means. I get to look at your expense report and see things that we are putting out when the public does."

Sean ran his hands through his hair. "We had to release some games because there was nothing in the queue. If you had some ideas and were running the company efficiently, then we wouldn't have an issue. Stop moping in the corner Simone, put on your big girl pants and come play in the sandbox."

Simone took a seat in front of his desk.

"You want to know what it looks like when I play with the big boys?"

"Simone, you really – "

"Just cut it, Sean. You want to take my company then go ahead you can have it. I'll do your dark web contracts, and you can control topside. You want the glory of it all. You want to be the man with all of the answers. The I.T man, fine. Let me help you."

Sean leaned closer to Simone. "The contracts are mine. You work for me. You better get that through your head. You see the problem with women is that it's always emotional. You better get this together, or you may have to worry about you, and what's your boy's name, David is it?"

"Sean, some things we don't cross the line on," Simone warned.

"If you believe that your still green Simone. You're not ready to play with the big boys. When it comes to money, you use every piece of leverage you have. Now listen to me, you do

whatever you have to do, but in two weeks' time I expect to see a working schedule of programs and any other new products for our other clients I expect their merchandise to be delivered in a timely fashion as usual."

Simone nodded her head and got up to leave the office. She turned right before leaving. "You know I can only do but so much. I suggest you talk to your workers. Also, you might want to live on the company it helps when you have issues like this."

"Live in the middle of nowhere; no thank you. This is about management. I don't' need to be there to manage. I just need to get you in line, and the rest will follow. I've earned my creature comforts, and I have no intention of staying on Sanctuary away from the real world. "

As Simone walked out the door, she said. "Everything has a price, make sure you can pay it, Sean."

CHAPTER THIRTY-TWO

Saturday night, Airport Hotel

Waking up to two men dragging you down a hallway and a woman leading the way never ended well for anyone. Jacob was impressed. He hadn't been in this situation for a while. He thought he had been careful, but he guessed it was true. Cockiness not only comes when you're young it can happen when you're older too. He didn't know what she had hit him with, but whatever it was it was gone. This was his curse and his blessing. He had a fast metabolism that nullified drugs on this system. Great skill to have when someone decides to snatch you. It's a curse when the doctor can't prescribe any meds and the only thing you can do is to go see someone's grandmother. And still the carpet went by, and not a soul came out of their hotel room.

So today it was the lights in the hallway that helped him focus on how bad the situation was. The woman opened his room door, and her friends dragged Jacob in.

Jacobs body had taken too long to recover. They were all in his room.

"I don't need all three. You two stay, and you go get everything prepared. I'll call in my update as soon as Jacob, and I come to an understanding."

'Well, the world hadn't gone completely crazy. Someone was sending a message. It means they didn't plan on killing him, just hurting him. It was looking up already.'

One of the guys dropped his hold on Jacob and walked out. Jacob tried to keep track of the guys. When the door closed, and he heard the footsteps from behind he had to make a move. He punched the guy holding his arm in the groin, put his knee down on the ground to stabilize himself and then pushed the moaning man back into the second guy by the door.

The second guy caught the first one and pushed him to the side. It gave Jacob just enough time to get to his feet.

"I thought he was out," the first man groaned while clutching himself and tried to stagger to his feet.

Jacob rammed his fist into the second guy's midsection. The second guy lurched forward with a groan and Jacob interlocked his hands and slammed it into the back of the second guy's head.

Jacob stood up and to make sure the guys were down and then he turned to the woman. Who stabbed him in the chest with three needles. The last thing he remembered was hearing her say "Playtime is over."

The darkness came and left the same way, in a riptide

of disorientation. It was the voice of the woman who had stabbed him in the chest.

"It's a good thing I brought extra to contain him. You are supposed to be the muscle, not me." Her hand was on his chest, and he could feel his arms had been tied to the bedpost and his ankles tied together.

"Open your eyes, Mr. Costa, we have business, and I don't have a lot of time."

Jacob didn't hesitate. He opened his eyes to see two angry goons standing at the end of the bed and the woman sitting next to him.

"My name is Jane Smith. You can call me Jane. We need you to find something of ours, 85 million dollars and some software."

"I don't know where it is," Jacob answered.

"This is one of those times I hope you're lying to me. We know Simone gave you the product. We believe she also gave you the money."

Jacob shook his head. "If you know it, someone lied to you. I don't have either."

Jane stood up and smoothed her dress down over her hips. "Let's try a different tactic. We know Simone left a message for you. Tomorrow you will get on a plane and get what she left you. After you retrieve it. You will bring it to me. Until we have that package, we will keep your family in Sanctuary." The third guy who had returned to the room pulled out two photos and handed it to Jane. She held them in front of Jacob. One was a picture of David sleeping in his room, and the other was a picture of Isabella sleeping on the couch in Peter's office.

"I'll leave these for you. We have the house locked down. When they wake in the morning, they'll know they can't get out. We can kill them in that house if we have to, but we are hoping it won't come to that. Find our money and bring it back to Sanctuary. We'll give you back your possessions, and we'll take ours." Jane promised.

"I know you are eager to get on with your task." Jane nodded to one of the guys, and they released one of his hands.

Jane smiled and leaned down over him. "Don't say I never did anything for you. With one hand you should be able to get out. Find my money and product Jacob, or you'll find your family in pieces." Jane stood up and blew him a kiss.

Jane walked away, but one of the men who came in with her took the opportunity to deliver a final blow to Jacob.

"Here's one to remember me by." Jacob couldn't move as he saw the descending fist. And after it hit him, he didn't see anything but darkness.

CHAPTER THIRTY-THREE

Sunday morning, Hotel Airport

He untied himself this morning and took a shower. It was time to go to California and pick up whatever Simone had left him. There was a knock on the door followed by a soft "excuse me cleaning lady."

Jacob opened the door to find his dead ex-wife swinging a serving plate at his head. Just in time, he brought his arm up to protect himself from the blow.

"What are you doing here! Leaving our boy alone and unprotected.?" She yelled. Jacob was trying to take in the fact it was dead Simone at his door. He backed into the room, and she advanced with her cart into his room. After he had deflected the serving pan twice, she rammed it into his stomach and then punched him. Neither stopped him. He charged her and pushed her back onto the bed.

"Our son is being held by those people because you let them get him!" she had balled up her fists and was hitting Jacob on his back. In between her tirade, Jacob caught her arms and put them above her head.

"Simone stop it! We need to figure this out not fight. He's our son, and I don't want anything to happen to him either." He said in between her blows.

Simone stopped swinging and started crying. Jacob let go of her arms, and she rolled onto her side. Her sobs echoed in the room. When Simone had calmed herself, she looked up at the ceiling and then turned to face Jacob who was lying next to her.

"Hate the circumstances, but long time no see." She said shaking her head.

He looked at her and laughed. "Is that all you have to say to me CeCe?"

Simone sat up, crossed her legs and looked at him. "You already know the important stuff. David is 8 years old."

"Where you going to tell me? I have a responsibility, and you were going to what? Tell him I didn't want him or maybe tell him someone else was his father?" Jacob asked.

Simone ran her hands through her short bob. Dressed all in black she looked fashionably chic. "I want to tell you I would have told you but I'm not sure. David is my life. He came when I didn't think I could care about anything."

"Why didn't you call me?"

"The truth Jacob. I didn't call you because I'm involved with people who don't play by the rules. I didn't know if you'd do whatever it took to make sure he was safe. I couldn't trust you not to get on your moral high horse and try to take my son."

"That's not – "

Simone held up her hand. "I'm sure someone would have come to you and said that he was in danger and the best thing was to put him in protective custody."

"With all of this going on- "

"That's not what's best for David. He can't be scurrying along all his life afraid. We need to eliminate the threat from his life."

"Eliminate?"

Simone stood up and paced the floor. "And here is the place where we separate. I don't have a problem with eliminating anything or one who might be a threat to David."

"What is it CeCe, you didn't think I would stand up for our son? The long-term problem is you don't think things through."

"No Jacob, I think you would do all the right things. Try to do it all the right ways. But my son doesn't have time for that. Whoever threatens him, should know they need to run and hide. I won't move my son, but I'll move any and everyone else."

Jacob stood up and tucked a curl around her ear. "That's always been the problem CeCe. It's always the extremes."

"No Jacob, you've forgotten where we came from. The people who act quickly and decisively live."

Jake cupped her cheek and ran his thumb over her cheek. "Who died in the crash, Cece?"

"Someone who wanted to die. They wanted to go, and I needed someone with matching dental records. I made sure their family had a good insurance policy, and that was that."

"CeCe – "

"No Jacob, I'm not like you. I don't think the good guys will win. When we met, I loved your honor and your belief in yourself, but I'm not like that. I don't think the world plays by those rules. I don't think they even know what honor is."

"So, you forgot what it means to have honor to CeCe? You let the world dictate who you are? Is that what you're teaching our son. To believe what they say about him and go out and prove it."

She turned away from him and went to the window.

"This conversation is going nowhere. I saw them take you from the bar last night. I watched, and they didn't bring out a body. So, I figured you were okay. What did Jane want?"

Jacob raised an eyebrow that she knew who Jane was. "They want the money. They think since you have sent me on this goose chase that you also gave me the money and the product."

"Well, at least that went well. I would rather have them coming after you and trying to kill you than to be hunting David and holding him for ransom."

"Do you think you could have asked me to participate in this? Why didn't you leave it with Sean?"

"Sean? Mr. Snake in the grass Sean? He wants to be Mr. Espionage and he can just not with my work."

"You know where the money and the code are?"

"Of Course, and we are going to get both. While we are going there, you can tell me about Isabella Nunez."

"Are you serious?" Jacob said.

"I want to know who you left to protect our son."

"CeCe Bella is- "Jake began.

"Oo Bella?" Simone teased.

"I call her that, but you know her name is Isabella. She's a good woman, and I'm happy I found her" Jacob said.

Simone reached out and touched his hand. "I'm glad you found what you were looking for. You are the best of guys Jacob. Just not the right kind of guy for me, then or now."

Simone picked up the serving platter and put it on the desk in the room. "However, let me be clear lover or no. Everyone is expendable for David. I'm hoping it doesn't come to that but if it does make sure you know which side you are on."

CHAPTER THIRTY-FOUR

We all fall down

It's never good news when the compliance officer calls the CEO of a company to the office. Roger was wondering who had been caught on what offense. It couldn't have been too important because the entire board had left today on a trip.

He knew they were going away to try to get rid of him and would try to use any excuse. This was probably one of the many bricks they had. It was one of the reasons his invite was delivered a few moments after the board had already left for their retreat.

Rogers went into Gaspers office. She was a plain looking woman. Straight black hair and no makeup. In order to get the particular shade of white Rogers knew she had to spend an inordinate amount of time using products to hide the freckles that still peeked through her pearl mask.

She looked up, and Rogers always felt as though she found him somehow lacking.

"Rogers," Gaspers said with a nod.

"Gaspers, what can I do for you?"

Gaspers reached to the corner of her desk and opened the manila folder.

"I don't require anything from you. This meeting is about you."

Rogers started to tense. This was the warning of the beginning of the end that Rogers knew was coming. Better that he finds out now.

She shuffled the papers one more time until she had the one she wanted and then she reviewed it before looking at Rogers.

"It has come to the board's attention that sales have been falling due to Safe Haven coming out with games similar in fashion to ours. After careful searching and due to evidence provided by a third-party source we have found you have been complicit with the opposition in giving away company plans."

Rogers stood up from the chair. "What evidence? I have the right to see the evidence that he has provided. And what third party source?"

"Actually, Rogers you do not have any rights in this situation. It is in the board regulations that if a third party approaches the board with enough information regarding an offense of this type. We do not have to engage you at all. It is left to the board to take immediate control and to make a decision in these situations where they will be made the sole executors of what is best for the company. These by-laws also state they can and will remove you from your position if they deem they are accurate, and the accusations are true."

"I'm being kicked out of my own company?"

"No, that decision has not been made as of yet. The board went away to discuss the situation. Right now, you are being *put on leave and still have your job but will not be involved in any decision making until the board returns with a verdict."*

"What about my rights?"

Gaspers pushed her black wire frame glasses up on her nose.

"The by-laws are clear. I would think you would understand them as they were voted on the last meeting and you agreed to them. An individual executive's rights can and will be revoked if it is deemed that the future of the company is at stake."

"So, what am I supposed to do now?" Rogers asked despondently.

"To be frank, in the short term, I would go home. In the long term, I suggest you evaluate your career options. The decision is not final, but the proof was conclusive."

"And the proof?"

Gaspers held up her hand and stopped the inquiry before Rogers could complete it. "The proof is none of your concern."

"It's frustrating not being able to refute when I don't know?"

"Refuting this proof would be challenging, but if you could explain the dropping sales and the way Safe Haven has come up with almost identical games, then the board would be open to listening to that." Gaspers offered.

Rogers walked out of Gaspers office and into the hall where two security officers were waiting for him. He looked over his shoulder to see Gaspers exiting her office.

"These guards will go with you to the office and assist you with getting any items you walked in here with this morning and then escort you to the front door."

Rogers grabbed his gear, and the guards escorted him to his car. When he called Sean's number, he got a disconnected number message from the message machine.

"No, no, no!" Rogers said as he hit the wheel of the car and he drove home. When he got to his home, he saw Carly outside getting into a car with her luggage. Rogers stopped on the street and got out of the car.

"Carly?"

"Oh, you're home early. I was hoping to avoid this."

"Avoid what?"

Carly reached out her hand and caressed his cheek before slapping him on it.

"Carly – "

"Don't. please don't. I'm tired, and I can't do this anymore. I knew it was going downhill but to have your friends call and think I'm one of those other women?"

"What – "

"Don't act surprised Sean called me and told me how you missed the plane with the other board members, to be with her. He thought I was her and offered to send me the ticket. When I told him that I wasn't the one you booked the ticket for, he hung up. I'm done."

Rogers watched Carly get into the taxi, and he sat on the curb. When she was gone from sight, he went to his car and dialed a number he never thought he'd use.

Sometimes when a rabbit gets caught by a wolf, the rabbit needs to run to a bigger, badder wolf.

The person answered on the second ring.

"You've reached the number of Simone Johns. I'm not available right now, but please leave your name and number."

CHAPTER THIRTY-FIVE

Sunday Morning, Orlando, Sanctuary

Isabella heard the birds, but everything was still dark. She had fallen asleep on the couch. She walked to the window, and the windows seemed dimmed as if they have a film across them. When Bella tried to open the window, nothing happened. She tugged again and still no movement. Then she heard Justice whimpering at the front door.

Isabella stepped away and listened. The house was silent. No breezes and no sounds. She ran out of the room and bumped into Peter. They both looked at one another and then said in unison. "David"

They took the steps and Isabella got to the door first. David was standing in the middle of the room with his superman backpack on.

David stopped and looked wide-eyed at both of them.

"I was going to tell both of you. Ms. Wise said we had to pack and go, honest I was going to tell you."

Isabella opened her arms. "Ms. Wise is wise, but in this case, she's late. Come here."

David ran into her arms. Isabella picked him up and took him downstairs. Isabella turned to Peter.

"I've checked the exits, but we can do it again."

They tried the windows in David room to find them all locked.

When they got to the first floor and went through each door, Isabella stopped with David in her arms. "Who builds a house that traps you!"

Peter grabbed David and went to his office. "The house was built as a safe house. Someone else has taken control of the house. And you build the feature in your home when you want to make sure no one will hurt the people in it."

"Well, where is the override for the house?"

"It should be in Simone's office."

As they walked out of his office and towards the office the, the green pad turned red. They both looked at each other and then went to Simone's door. Peter put his hand on the panel, and nothing happened. The scanner stayed red.

"Keys?" Bella asked.

Peter shook his head." The lock is a dummy lock. It doesn't do anything or go anywhere. This room is specifically built for this occurrence and linked with the electronics in the house.

David lifted his head from Peter's shoulder. "I'm sorry. I should have told you Ms. Wise said to Pack and go."

Isabella reached out and smoothed his hair over his head. "We'll be fine David."

As David lay his head back on Peter, Isabella caught Peter's eyes.

"Well, we know this, Simone's office turned red when we went towards it."

"Yes?" Peter replied.

"It means this house has eyes," Isabella said.

CHAPTER THIRTY-SIX

Sunday Morning, Simone's house

"Ms. Owl has something to say," David said.

Both Isabella and Peter stopped. Isabella picked up David and held him to her chest.

"David, I know – "

"I can take you to the safe place." David interrupted Isabella. He wiggled down and went up the stairs. Isabella followed him wondering where this was going. David had been telling them about Ms. Owl for all the time she had been here. The only noise in the house was the scratching of Justice's nails on the floor.

When they went into his room, David told them both to sit on the bed. He went into the closet and then came out.

"Okay, we're alone," David said as he sat at his desk.

"David, why do you think we are safe?" Isabella asked.

"One-day mommy came home and said there were

eyes in the house. I remembered when you said it today. She set up a switch in the room, so no one would see me. It was our secret." David said puffing his chest up.

Peter laughed out loud. "That's my girl. This is all making sense now."

Isabella turned to Peter looking bewildered. If you have had some sort of epiphany, please feel free to share the moment."

Peter went to kneel in front of David. "Did mommy give you Ms. Owl too?"

David smiled "Yes she did. She told me it would take care of me. "

"David earlier you said Ms. Owl said it was time to pack and go."

David nodded his head.

"Did she really tell you?"

"Yes, she did! I told the truth. It was after read me my story." David said.

Isabella looked at the stuffed owl. "There is no way; this could be true. It's straight out of some old movie."

Peter smiled at Isabella. "Welcome to my life with Simone. "

Peter went into the closet and looked around. Isabella could hear him grunting inside. "Hand me your phone Isabella."

"I don't have a dial tone. I checked earlier."

"I don't want to make a call; I need the light."

Isabella handed the phone over to him. After a few more moments Peter came out of the room with a smile on his face.

"The switch is hooked up to a camera that runs a feedback loop on the camera."

"What?" Isabella said.

"She knew someone was watching her. She installed the camera to show the last minute over and over in the room."

"You think she would have told you something like that," Isabella said sarcastically.

"I assume she kept me in the loop just as much as Jacob does for you." Peter sniped back.

Isabella looked at the toy. "Well, I've got nothing to lose with this next step. David can I hold Ms. Owl for a moment."

David looked at her skeptically. "You'll give her back to me, right?"

"Yes David, I will I just want to see if Ms. Owl will talk to me."

Bella turned to look into the owl's face and waited. The owl's eyes were closed When nothing happened she hung her head. "I've been here too long, and this is beyond crazy."

David started laughing "You didn't say anything."

Peter took the owl. "Simone"

The eyes opened. Isabella leaned over and looked at the toy. "Well at the very least, the eyes opened for you." She said

"I can feel some pads on the back of the toy. It has a number pad on the back." Peter said.

David jumped up and down with a mischievous smile on his face. "I know, I know. Mommy told me Ms. Owl is holding her greatest project and that's why I had to hold on to Ms. Owl because I'm mommy's best thing she ever created."

"Well, lookie there, it's all about the questions you ask. "Said, Isabella.

Peter looked into the eyes of the toy and started to speak.

"Simone are you in there?"

For a few moments there was nothing, and then the owl blinked its eyes. "Of course."

CHAPTER THIRTY-SEVEN

Peter asked." Are you okay?"

"Living"

Peter asked the doll. "Simone we're trapped in the house."

"Too late said run"

"We can't get into the office. Any ideas" Peter asked.

"Maybe load circuits back door open."

"Are you with Jacob?" Isabella asked.

"Yes"

Isabella sat back and let out a breath and little sob. She had been worried about him ever since he hadn't answered the text.

"Not long both will be here soon," Simone said.

"I'll work on a way to secure the channel and make communication a little smoother," Isabella said.

"Do you have the money or the code?" Peter asked.

"Get money now, David code," Simone answered.

Isabella heard the doll but couldn't believe it. At that moment she and Peter were in the same state of disbelief.

"Simone needs to say it again I think we got it wrong. Where is the code?"

"Code in Owl's back. Don't give code all die."

"What kind of foolishness is this?!" cried Isabella.

"She's amazing," Peter said as Ms. Owl closed her eyes.

"She's amazing! She's crazy! We are going around here risking our lives; there are crazy people trying to steal David and all the time the answer was sitting in the heart of the doll. What kind of mother does this?"

"The kind that's willing to do anything for her child. If we had given the code to anyone, they would have taken David to get the money anyway. When we have both, we'll be able to bargain or draw them out, so David will be safe."

Isabella took a long look at Peter.

"Did you know she had the code?"

"I didn't know, but I'm not surprised."

"I asked you to be upfront with me."

"I told you I'd give you what I could, and I did. I did what you would do for Jacob."

Isabella looked away. She didn't have anything to say. Peter said the truth, for Jacob she'd keep her silence on her speculations if she thought it would protect Jacob. To make sure a child was okay, she'd go the extra mile. She didn't blame him. She just couldn't put it into perspective while everyone's life was on the line. She knew if anything happened to Jacob, she wouldn't be able to forgive him either.

CHAPTER THIRTY-EIGHT

Sunday Morning,

Sean woke reached over to his night table and picked up his phone. He did what he did every morning; he checked his bank account. There were three more "donations" made during the night. If this was the pattern, he would be donating about 500,000 a day.

If he could kill Simone again, he would. He didn't really believe the only one who could get rid of the virus was this supposed spider. That's what he had all of those mules on the floor beneath him come in early. They had been working on the code since he left the building last night.

His bank account was still dwindling which meant they hadn't been able to break it either. Nothing had gone the way it was supposed to with Simone. She hadn't followed the plan. He hadn't expected her to give everything to her ex and he certainly hadn't expected her to die.

He was smarter than her, wasn't he?

Morning was coming, and the bright sky was rolling with full clouds that gathered waiting for the best time to unleash the storm in them. Cool air buffeted the curtains in his place. He picked up the phone and called Jane.

The phone rang once.

"Jane" she answered.

"Where are you?" Sean asked.

"I'm at the airport waiting for your package."

"I need you to do something while you're babysitting," Sean said.

"Hmm"

"I need to find a coder named the spider. I have a virus on my machine. I gift from Simone, and I need someone to stop it.

"We could try to get – "

"Don't think! It's a useless activity for us both. Can you find the spider or not?"

There was a silence on the other line and then and exhaled breath.

"I can find him. I think I know but let me confirm with my sources." Jane said.

"I've also asked Rogers to look, but I don't know if I have as much confidence in him as I use to. He couldn't close the deal with Jacob, and he let himself get fooled by Simone in the past. And while we are talking about failures. Rogers will have to be dealt with after we've gotten the money and the merchandise."

"Of course, Mr. Carstairs."

"Good, find that spider and let me know," Sean said as he hung up the phone. He didn't wait to hear what she said. He knew he paid enough to get blind obedience.

CHAPTER THIRTY-NINE

Sunday 11.00 a.m., Simone's house

Isabella woke to a chill in the air.

They decided to turn the cameras back on and calm David down. After Ms. Owl spoke, he wanted nothing but his mother. Peter and Isabella laid with him until he drifted off. They held David and David held Ms. Owl. All of them were waiting. Peter was against the wall, David was in between them and Justice laid across everyone's feet. Ms. Owl had not decided to talk after that moment with Peter. Isabella wasn't sure if she was happy or sad.

David cuddled a little closer to her and murmured. "I'm cold, Isabella."

Bella looked at Peter, and he was already awake. Bella mouthed 'I'll be back.' "I'll go downstairs to check the thermostat." Peter nodded, and David turned to snuggle with Peter.

Rolling from the bed, she left the room and went

downstairs. She found the thermostat, and it was electric. At first, she wasn't sure if it was working and tried pressing the buttons, but nothing happened. Next to the thermostat was the intercom. First, she heard a crackling from it and then she heard his voice.

"Hello Isabella, it's been a long time since I met a coder I wanted to play with."

Isabella stood still and didn't let the wave of panic take over.

"It seems a little unfair you know my name, and I don't know yours," she said.'

"It's John. Not that it will matter to you anyway."

"John, why are you keeping us here?"

"Insurance. Your boy needs to get some things for me, and then we'll release everyone."

Bella heard the snicker in his voice and had no doubt he didn't intend for any of them to make it all.

"We need the thermostat turned up," Isabella said.

"Maybe, maybe not. You don't get to say what happens here, I do."

Isabella tried to trace the line of the thermostat to see where it led.

"Good thinking Isabella but where you need access to is the outside of the house."

Isabella had a thought.

She went to the guest bedroom and looked around. She had left the bed in a hurry. She went to the closet and then packed up some warm clothes to take to David. John never left her alone.

"That's right Isabella; you better get some covers it's

going to get a lot colder for you all. I can see you, so I'll make sure you don't die too soon."

Bella got her robe and threw it over her laptop on the book. She rolled up the comforter and took it to David's room. When she got to the room, Peter sat up and looked at her and the items she carried with a raised brow.

"Safe space" Bella mouthed.

Peter got up as if he were helping Bella and then opened the closet and turned on the camera inside.

"Okay, why did you bring these?"

"Look he's got eyes on us, and when I went to turn off the thermostat there's no access to the wires," Isabella said.

Peter waved his hand in a rolling motion "And – "

"And what that means is there has to be at least one signal going out because he has to be using it to send a signal in."

Bella dug her computer out of the covers and booted up. She looked for the WIFI and then began to look for mac addresses of the cameras. The cameras id told her where they were. One by one she took over the cameras. The one in David's room was first. Then the one by the front door.

"What are you doing Isabella?"

She could hear the anger in John's voice. She kept finding the cameras hijacking them and making them show black as if they had been disconnected. When she was all done, she looked up and heard John screaming throughout the house.

"What have you done to my cameras?! Don't make this harder than you need to. You can't get out!"

David rolled over on the bed and rubbed the sleep out of his eyes.

"What happened why is all this stuff in my room?" Justice crawled up closer to David and rested her big head on his lap.

"We just made the bad guy blind David; now we have to find a way to look through his eyes."

"Can you do that?" Peter asked.

"I can do that, and hopefully we can find a way out," Isabella said.

CHAPTER FORTY

Jacob saw a cab in front of the hotel. He hailed it and then got in. Just when they were about to pull out, there was a double tap on the back of the car.

"What?" Jacob said as he turned to see who had tapped the taxi.

Cece got in the car.

"Lady I've got a fare." The driver said.

"it's no problem." Jacob waved away the concerns of the driver.

The cabby shrugged his shoulders and then took off.

Jacob looked at Cece. "What are you doing?"

"Making sure our son is fine. Your girlfriend is pretty smart, but I don't know how long they are going to play with them in the house."

"You spoke to her?"

"No, but I have some ways to check in on them."

He wanted to reach out and strangle her. "When were you going to mention this?'

Cece stopped and looked at him. "I wasn't and if you want to know why look at yourself now. If I had told you earlier, you would have wanted to contact her, and I don't know how long I'll be able to keep this connection secret."

Jacob could only think about how Isabella had sent him the last message. He couldn't call, and she hadn't called him. There was a wave of guilt for leaving Isabella. They hadn't worked out everything, and she was trapped in a house with his son.

"She's fine by the way. She asked about you, and I told her you fine as well. See I can be a feeling person sometimes." Simone said defiantly.

Jacob remembered just last week they had taken a picture with Justice and framed it and called it their family. Now he was sitting with CeCe and Isabella was unprotected and in danger because of him.

"Jacob, I need you to go to our bed and breakfast we went to. I've already bought your ticket, so expect for Ms. Jane to show up. They think you know where the money is. The only thing is if you talk to Jane, ask her who she's working for."

"CeCe do we know where the money is?"

"Yes"

"You've spoken to them; I need to speak to Isabella." Jacob insisted.

"Jacob, you need to keep moving so they can stay alive," she replied. "The buyer representatives will be looking to you to bring them to their money, or we won't see either of them alive."

"Did you see them? Did you – "

"I talked to them and few words at that. When the buyer comes, and they will tell them you want to talk to them. Or ask for some proof that they're okay."

Jacob nodded. The buyer had his family. He didn't know who to trust besides Cece. And trusting Cece was like having faith. You got no reassurances, and it wouldn't make sense until the very end. So, he'd wait for Jane to show up because at this moment she was the only one he knew might be able to give him an update on his family.

CHAPTER FORTY-ONE

Sunday afternoon, Simone's home

We have to find a way to hunt him.

After turning the cameras dark, all of them moved out of the closet. Peter, David, and Justice resettled themselves on the bed under the covers. For now, they could deal with the cold. Isabella needed to know who their enemy was.

Peter looked at Isabella while David was cradled in his arms. David snuggled to get warm, and Peter nodded.

"Tell me you have some more tricks in that laptop of yours," Peter said with a smile.

"You're taking this really well." She said.

"What else is there to do? Until we have an idea who we are dealing with, we have to wait," Peter sighed.

"How long have you known about Simone?"

Peter let out a heavy sigh and then went back to rocking David to sleep as Justice lay her head in David's lap. "In truth, I didn't know at all. I suspected something wasn't right a couple of days before her accident. It would have been useless to ask Simone, so I waited."

"And you? How long have you been hiding your abilities from Jacob?"

Bella smiled warily at Peter. "I'm not sure I understand."

"I thought we had gotten closer than that Isabella. I met Jacob. I've talked to him and made a plan to save a child who may or may not be his. He is a man of high moral. You are saving us and breaking into things with a lot more familiarity than a programmer who does this for a hobby. I was one of the people behind the walls. It looks like you were good enough never to get caught."

"Maybe I'm a genius problem solver." Isabella sniped

"I have no doubt you're a genius. How long?"

"I keep my skills up, but I used to do this to get through college. It gave me quick cash, and as long as no one was hurt, it didn't seem so bad."

"I hear a story in there?"

"I know about boutiques because I was offered a job by one. They let me do a trial for a week. It was amazing; it was fast. The money was more than I had seen, and I figured out how to manage the dark web without a problem."

"It sounds like everything you were looking for."

"When you surf the web, you realize everything is for sale. Human trafficking as well."

"Ah, so you and Jacob do share some a very moral

backbone." He chuckled.

"I'm not saying I'm better than anyone!"

"No, but you were offended by the wares?"

"I couldn't live with myself working in that world," Isabella said.

"Then you picked the right person staying with Jacob and Jacob picked the right woman."

"Peter if you had seen – "

Peter reached out and touched Bella's hand. "You don't have to tell me. I work on that web every day. But I have seen the best and worst of people. Remember family dropping me in prison for my brother to have a chance at getting a seat."

Looking at David and then to Peter. "Then how do you work in that world when you have David?"

"It's because of David that I'm there. Simone and I decided that because there were people like that, we couldn't afford to be prudish. We had to be around them, to track them."

"But – "

"We can argue later. You wanted to hunt, remember?"

Shaking her head, she nodded yes. "Let's see if this will work. It's an old trick, but here goes."

She logged onto google and then typed in a line in the search engine, and pages and pages came back. Some of it wasn't even in English. She ran a search for the MAC addresses that she had found when she turned the cameras dark. She found one and clicked on the link.

A blank white page showed first. Then on the right

side four buttons with the directional arrows of up, down, left and right appeared. The arrows were on blue buttons and below that showed a number pad. On the right side, an image window opened. It showed a room with a chair.

Peter leaned a little closer to the laptop. "What is this?'

"I found one of the cameras that are in this house and instead of him looking at us we are looking at him. The controls on the side allow me to move it right or left. I'm hoping I can see who it is, so we can know who we are dealing with."

Isabella moved the remote to the left and saw nothing. Then she moved it to the right, and there was a refrigerator. A man was in it getting something out. She pushed the middle button that was circular in the middle of the directional buttons and it zoomed in. When the man turned around Peter spoke.

"I can't believe it. It's the slow maintenance guy."

"Humph, he's not as slow as you think. Looking at this equipment. He's been here awhile. I think that's enough."

Isabella closed the camera and exited the google screen. She turned to Peter.

"Okay, tell me everything you know about this guy, where he lives and what you think you know about him. Let's see if we can get him to make a move or find some other way out." Isabella said.

Peter looked at Ms. Owl. "I wanted to wait and plan with Simone, but I know she'll agree to save David first."

"Well my thought is this, we'll hope there's good news, but we need to get ourselves out if we can. The cavalry might come too late." Isabella said.

CHAPTER FORTY-TWO

"I'm here to pick up my ticket. Can I do that here?" Jacob asked.

"Yeah, hold on." The clerk said.

The man behind the airlines counter looked at Jacob with a cynical look, after a couple of taps on his terminal he looked up.

The young man was thin, and Jacob didn't think this was the first job option for him. His tendency to roll his eyes and his curt tone.

"Your name and your destination."

"Jacob Costa to Monterey."

The young man glanced down again at his terminal and typed away again.

"Wow, someone must like you, you have a first-class ticket."

"Good things come when you least expect it," Jacob said.

"I'll need your identification please?"

It was the first time Jacob had heard him use the word, please. It made him wonder if his first-class ticket gave him the privilege of kindness. Jacob gave his two pieces of Id, his driver's license, and his work license.

The young man laughed. "Are you serious, it says you're a penetration specialist. What is that?"

The young man leered at him and leaned a little closer. Jacob knew all of the jokes when people heard his job title. He didn't want to be educating the hormonally imbalanced and miss his flight.

"It's not what you think. It means that I break into computers all day long."

"That's a computer job? I can do that."

"Without getting caught going in or coming out. Do you work with computers outside of here?'

"No, I do moving art."

"That's got to be fun."

"Yeah, you sound like my parents," the man laughed. "I hope you have fun and at the very least you've got a great job title."

Jacob laughed, shook his head and took the ticket. His job title was the number one icebreaker when he went to see clients or give lectures. Jacob looked at the time and found the gate. There wasn't much time before the flight would board. So much had happened these last two days and there was still more to do. He hadn't had time to process the situation.

His ex-wife wasn't dead, his current lover was trapped in a house with his son, and he needed to find money and code for an illegal boutique. When he reviewed how this all happened.

Jacob tried to think of how he was going to get them all out. He would find the money, and the code would be retrieved. He was confident Isabella would be okay. She was an amazing woman, and if there was a way to keep them both alive, Isabella would do it. Simone was just as dedicated to making sure their son survived.

He knew an opportunity would come. H didn't see it yet but that was fine, the answer would come, and he'd be ready for it when it did.

CHAPTER FORTY-THREE

Mr. Knight was patient; he had to be. For the last ten years, he had been trying to catch the simple man. The Simple man had released a ransom virus in the hospitals, and the city had been brought to its knees trying to figure it out. Knight was never any good when it came to working with computers, but he started out as a good cop and now worked in the FBI according to the official records. Knight and his wife had been married for 13 years.

Sarika Knight was mighty at 5'6". She was a nurse with a soft voice and a gentle touch. When she met Knight, she saw past his gruff Jamaican disposition and loud antics to see the man. She never asked for him to change and she loved him unconditionally.

When the ransom virus was discovered, it was the hospital Sarika was working in. She wasn't even a full-time nurse at the hospital. She was a per diem for the day. The fact that Sarika was worried pushed Knight to go even harder in finding the simple man. While the geeks did their thing, Knight did his. He looked through receipts, tracked down where the simple man bought supplies. Locating empty realty buildings and finding several homes that were up for sale, but electricity was being used by clusters of programmers who could never identify the simple man but knew he funded their operation. He put his nose to the grindstone and narrowed it down to three houses.

Before he left, he called Sarika. She was exhausted. All patient information had to be manually entered. Sarika was teaching the fresh staff how to use paper while she was making sure that her patients were okay.

"Sari I've almost got him."

"I knew you would Knight. You're my shining knight."

"Get ready to come home. You've been working too much."

"We serve knight, and I'm always happy to serve you."

"Sari save your strength as I'll be collecting on that service card you be handing out."

Sarika laughed. A couple of beeps went on in the background. She sighed. "Go save the world. Remember, I love you."

"I love you too."

Knight hung up and then called his partner. They had looked in the first house and found nothing and then Knight had a hunch about the second one. They approached the house, and they entered the house in a textbook fashion. They did it by the numbers and found the computer. On the computer, he had left the code to fix the ransomware. Knight shook his head and told his partner to call it in, so they could get the answer to the geeks at the station.

Knight turned the paper over with the answer, and there was one line.

"It's simple; you can't be in more than one place at a time. Mr. Knight"

Knight looked at the message and then ran to the car. He dialed Sarika while he was driving. He knew Sarika was in the emergency room. She had moved off of her floor from pediatrics and offered to help in the emergency room. When Sarika didn't answer, he dropped the phone as soon as he was on the same block as the hospital. Just as he pulled up to the lane, the explosion rocked the emergency room.

Knight couldn't remember getting out of the car. He couldn't remember fighting the authorities on site. The last thing he remembered was when they brought out her body. He was numb as they loaded her into the ambulance and when he sat in his car to follow his phone rang.

"See Knight life is simple."

From that day on Knight had made it his priority to work under the radar but always on catching the simple man. He knew what he was going to do when he caught him. Sarika's memory demanded no less. He could walk away from his career, but he couldn't walk away from Justice for Sarika.

The simple man was hard to track. Now he had finally come out for software that could clear the airways. He'd waited all of this time; Knight could wait a little longer.

It was the least he could do for Sarika

CHAPTER FORTY-FOUR

Enemies can be Friends

Roger had closed the door to his office and contemplated killing himself or trying to rebuild. His wife wasn't with him for love, and she was his ticket to old money parties. His accounts were dwindling, and Sean had used him for what he wanted and now had cast him aside. At one time he thought he was going to be partners with Sean. Now he realized Sean had already taken his company and made him an employee.

He thought he could rebound. Roger had told his wife it was a new position. She hadn't pressed him, but when her car had been declined at a shop, she told him to pull it together. Roger looked at the paper check in his hand and the note attached.

"Your services will no longer be needed."

When he had received it this morning, he went into frantic mode. He read it several times and tried to call Sean on all the numbers he had. Finally, he had just sat outside of Nova headquarters until Sean had come out.

Sean walked over to him smiling. He knew he had been out here waiting. He knew all along.

Roger stood up, and Sean spoke first. "I'm surprised you stayed out here that long. You're persistent, but you lack long-term planning."

"What did I do to deserve this Sean?"

"You see Roger. It's not about deserving. It's about the strong taking what they want and the weak falling to the side or being eaten. You and Simone just weren't meant to be at the top."

Roger wasn't sure what he could do, but there was something he had to try. Calling Simone was a risk. He wasn't sure she would even take his call. He didn't call from the company phone, he called from his home or at least it was for now. He wanted her to know who was on the other line. The time for hiding was over anyway. He had called before and left a message. He was hoping she'd be there tonight.

On the first ring, he started to think he was foolish. On the second ring, he knew he was setting himself up for failure. On the third ring, he couldn't even imagine the words he would say. Then she picked up.

"I'll give you credit for having the grit to call me back, Roger."

"It wasn't grit. It was desperation." Said, Roger.

She didn't sound like the woman whose company he had helped to steal. There was no bitterness in her voice.

"And yes, it's me, Roger," he said. He was so lost. There was a time he spoke with authority. He had the urge to hang up, but he kept thinking about Sean's smile.

"I'm sure you didn't call to tell me your name, so what do you want Roger." Roger sat up a little straighter. She knew it was him and they were still talking sort of. She didn't sound like any angry woman he knew, and, so he pressed forward.

"I called to talk to you because Sean double crossed me and took my company. I thought maybe you could help me."

The next thing he heard was Simone laughing. This was what he had expected. She'd ridicule him and then hang up. She stopped laughing after a minute and then paused.

"You're serious?!"

"Yes." He said in a voice low

He heard a long pause and waited for the excuse for her to get off the phone. Instead, she asked a question.

"Okay, Roger tell me why you really called?"

"Sean threw me away. I don't have much, and I don't have anything or any other options. On top of that, Sean told Carly that I was cheating."

"I'm a crossroads here Roger. My first instinct is to laugh at you and tell you I told you so. Then I think of Sean and how he can trick anyone, and then I feel sorry for you. Even when both of those run its course I have to think; I don't know if I can actually do anything for you."

Roger knew it already. He just needed to confirm how lost things were. The gun was looking like a better option.

"Are you still working?"

He thought he would save himself the humiliation of how low he'd fallen but right now he didn't have time for pride. "No, he gave me a check."

"The word is he's already sold your company to a shadow company that needed a front. The best I can do is get you back in that door. I hear the owner is eccentric, and doesn't spend a lot of time in the office but will need someone to run the business."

Roger swallowed hard. "Why?"

Simone laughed. "Why am I helping you? I think because we all make mistakes and we should learn from them if we can. A man I knew used to tell me that. Besides this being a mother thing can soften you up. But I'm not completely altruistic. I want something."

"Name it; I can do it."

"I want a favor for the future."

"Are you doing something now?"

"No, not now but I'm a patient woman."

"I didn't think I'd be saying this when I picked up this phone but when you need something, call me."

"We're not getting married. I'm keeping you on a string, and I'm going to yank it later on. Until then, live your life and enjoy your family. We'll be in touch."

Simone was sneaky, but tonight she had become an ally and he couldn't wait for the day she called. He needed to try to get his life back together. Roger didn't know what Simone would ask but whatever it was he'd pay later.

CHAPTER FORTY-FIVE

The reason why people sought revenge is because it feels so good. Sean had no doubt that Roger was incompetent but sometimes he actually produced, and the donations were increasing from his account.

"Sean, I found the person with special talents."

Sean didn't like Roger calling him. As he sat at his desk he could almost see Roger salivating over his present condition. Sean wasn't naive when it came to working with Roger. He knew Roger worked for his old company. Sean had gone to Roger with the opportunity to get Safe Haven and get back at Simone Johns. All that being said it didn't mean he trusted him at all.

"Good," Sean said trying to keep any form or want out of his voice.

"Well, I'm glad you asked me. I want to do something to repay you. I admit I'm not as well connected as I once was but there are some people I made sure to keep in contact with," Roger stated.

Sean decided that he would kill Roger after this call. Maybe he'd ask Jane to record his death on her phone and send it to him.

"You know I've got Simone's old machine. Jacob was looking for it and he had the password to it." Fortunately, I saved it.

"Ah", Roger commented.

Sean pushed on. "I had to connect the machine to a network and I put in the password. The password let me into the first level and then it connected to my machine. I entered the information and it continued on"

"That seems so typically Simone," Roger added.

"Well it was typically Simone, treacherous. Then it connected to my personal accounts. It has been sending out donations from me to children organizations in everything from 100 to 40,000 dollars."

"How often?"

"Every 4 hours." Sean bit out.

"The lady knows how to leave an impression," Roger stated.

"So, you found 'The Spider'.

"I'd heard of him before, but I'd never dealt with him due to his list of demands." Roger claimed.

"Like – "Sean prodded.

"He doesn't travel. You have to go meet him. I can give you an address. The way it works is you have to go to a hotel. Leave a message for him at the front desk and wait. If you haven't been contacted in 5 hours, then you know he's not going to take your case." Roger said.

Sean pulled the phone away from his head and

imagined skinning Roger instead of letting Jane kill him.

"You seem to be really familiar with this person." Sean's distrust making him skeptical about the tale.

"When I had a company, I use to have some issues that I could refer to him. He didn't always take on the cases I threw to him but when he did I was happy. The downside is the price tag afterward. He doesn't talk to the customer, instead he does his own research and finds out how valuable the job is and then charges accordingly."

Sean listened to Roger and he barely contained his frustration to have to depend on this man. It sounded like the Spider was a businessman thank goodness. Great talent always set itself aside. It seemed like the Spider just wanted to be compensated. Sean understood that and would be more than willing.

"By the nature of the problem, you did convey to him that I won't be able to bring the hardware with me?"

"Yes, he will see you and if he can take on the case he will make the arrangements to access the information. He'll send instructions after he accepts the case, if he takes the case on." Roger said.

"The hotel?" Sean asked.

"It's the Monterey Plaza Hotel. When you get to the front desk tell them your name and tell them you have a message for the Widow."

"A bit dramatic don't you think?" Sean commented

"The rumors say the Spider has done some impressive and borderline illegal fixes. I toss it up to an occupational hazard."

"Thanks Roger."

"Sean, I owed you. If it weren't for you I wouldn't be here. The opportunity with Costa was a last chance. I don't need to like you to be able to see opportunity." Rogers said.

They hung up and Sean looked at the phone. He would go to Monterey see if Simone left anything he could use. If luck was good he'd get the code and a hint about the money. At a minimum he'd get some code and resell it.

Jacob and Peter could deal with the simple man and try to protect the boy. He wouldn't like it, but Sean was going to cut his losses. He'd sell whatever was on Simone's machine and think about his next move. Maybe he'd lay a trail to Roger as well and let the simple man take care of him instead of Jane.

He always came out on top, or at least he was never on the bottom.

CHAPTER FORTY-SIX

Redemption

They were seated around the board table with their tails between their legs. None of them could meet her eye and she walked in like royalty.

"Hello Ms. Johns, we're so glad you could make time in your schedule. We were hoping to present an opportunity to you."

Oh, how times change, not so long ago they were ready to forget my name and now look at them, she thought.

Melvin Travane cleared his throat and gestured for her to sit.

"Please Ms. Johns have something to drink."

Mr. Travane, who knew he could be so accommodating thought Simone.

"Hello Ms. Johns, I hope this meeting hasn't inconvenienced you. We have been very impressed with your performance and wanted to make sure you were appreciated.," he said as he eyed each of the board members at the table.

The only thing missing from this room from her last encounter was Sean Carstairs.

"After evaluating our holdings and the performance of some of our other properties it has come to our attention that an associate of ours, Mr. Carstairs has not been as productive or forthcoming in his dealings with us"

"Really? I thought Mr. Carstairs was a good friend of the board," she murmured quietly.

"It's come to light that Mr. Carstairs may have competing interests with the board" he said. A couple of the board members cleared their throats or looked away when Mr. Ravine spoke.

"I see." Simone said in her most demure voice possible.

"Yes, Mr. Carstairs is rethinking his future plans. He has left for an opportunity. That has left a new opening, that we feel you are more than qualified for."

Gathering himself to his full height he nodded to the board.

"We'd like you to know your hard work has been noticed."

"For the past two quarters you've been in charge of the company quarter earnings. We've seen a significant increase in profits. Your primary competitor Learning Technologies has gone to the wayside leaving Safe Haven at the top of your field." A board member commented.

"Quarters come and go, Ms. Johns. We are interested in promoting those who do excellent work." Mr. Travane said

"Forgive me gentlemen, but the last time I was here it was your opinion that I wasn't fit to run Safe Haven. It seems your opinion has changed. I want you to know that I still have a son. I'm still a mother."

Simone curled her hands around the coffee cup. She had to

keep her cool and her temperament. She had worked to bring this day about and it was for David. It was all for David.

"In regards to our last meeting, we would like to put that behind us. We are hoping you will also be able to do that as well. We are all human, but we have the same end cause, to make a profit." Mr. Travane said.

"I agree." Simone said.

Mr. Travane's smile widened and he continued.

"I knew you would be reasonable. We would like you to run Safe Haven.".

Travane had the smile on his face that David had when he got what he wanted. Simone wanted to pat him on the head and tell him good boy, but she contained herself.

"While I am flattered that you have found me worthy to lead Safe Haven. I need to look out for my son and me. So, I would be honored to take the position as long as I have some conditions met."

Travane cleared his throat and then sat closer to the board table. "Ms. Johns, most people would just take the offer. It doesn't seem very professional of you to have conditions."

Simone smiled at Travane and looked around the table.

"Gentlemen, I want full control over Safe Haven. Since Mr. Travane has brought up professionalism let me also add transparency. I don't want any of the profits that Safe Haven makes on the 'web'. I'm only interested in what Safe Haven the toy company does. As a mother I want to be able to secure his future. The bulk of the money you are impressed with comes from the web. I think it's a small thing to give me Safe Haven and you keep the other portion."

One of the members cleared his throat. You'd relinquish

your rights to all of it?"

"Yes" she said.

There were some murmurings around the table.

Travane leaned over and spoke to a member next to him as well. Travane nodded to the other members.

"Ms. Johns your request is as unconventional as you are. We agree. We will give you Safe Haven and you will run its sister company without any compensation from the company providing services on the web."

Simone stood up with a large smile on her face.

"Gentlemen thank you. I've waited a long time to have my own company and I want to thank you for sticking with me and having faith in my abilities."

"We'll send the appropriate paperwork."

Simone nodded. "Thank you and my son thanks you as well."

CHAPTER FORTY-SEVEN

Meeting at the crossroads
Sean walked into the office and saw Simone sitting behind the desk.
"Sean."
"Simone. Congratulations."
"This isn't about winning and losing. I just want to make sure my son is taken care of and that I can live with myself."
Sean harrumphed. "It's always about winning and losing Simone. You can't protect the world from itself. I figured if the world wants to mess its future up why not make a profit?"
Simone went to Sean.
"You could make a difference and not add to the problem. There are a lot of things on the web that we should be trying to fight."
Sean looked at Simone and shook his head.
"I didn't look deep enough Simone."
Simone was confused. "I don't understand.'

"You still believe in people. I thought Jacob had cured you of that, but I guess not. For now, enjoy but people will disappoint you and your principles will hamper you in the long term.

Sean walked out of her office. She wished Sean was irrational, but he seemed level headed. She wanted to believe that this was the end, but she knew Sean. If she was honest with herself, she would say she was Sean, before David.

This wouldn't be the last time she saw Sean, which meant she needed to prepare.

CHAPTER FORTY-EIGHT

It had taken seven and half hours to bring him back in time to this room. When Simone had said she left the hint in this hotel, Jacob thought for sure she had picked another room. He should have known better, this was the same room they had their wedding night.

Jacob was standing in front of the hotel room with his electronic key. He waved it in front of the lock and opened up to memories. The room had cost 500 a night. It was the most expensive room he had ever had to pay for and right after the wedding. He was numb to what the fuss was about but, Simone loved it.

"Jacob look it's got that old-world elegance to it. Look when you walk in there's a vanity for me to look at myself."

Jacob walked down the narrow hall into the sitting area. "Well it's got two balconies." He remembered saying.

Jacob remembered Simone saying, "Jacob look here in

the closet they not only have a robe, but they've also got sandals in here too."

Jacob laughed at the memory. Then he had told Simone "Shoes, for the price we are paying they should offer me some real shoes as well."

Jacob walked onto a balcony and looked at the bay. When he looked, he saw the boats already taking people on what Simone had called a poor man's cruise. Jacob turned back into the room and looked at the bland artwork and the comfortable sofa.

He looked around trying to see if there was anything that would give him a clue and stop him from going down memory lane. He searched the sitting room, moving pictures on the walls and rearranging the furniture. When he went into the bedroom. Inside there were two more balconies. There was coordinated linen on the King-sized bed. The balconies opened to the docks across the way.

He picked up the binoculars that were on the reading table by the balcony door. Simone had thought the binoculars were a great touch. Jacob thought the binoculars were just another way to justify the price.

Jacob hadn't really cared for the whole experience, but it wasn't for him. Simone wanted to live the dream and be a princess. She said she was only going to marry once. They had picked the state together, but she had picked the hotel.

Jacob had looked at honeymoon suites, but Simone wanted to be in the 'executive suite'. She said you had to live today how you wanted to live tomorrow. He thought she was crazy then, but now he could see she had gotten what she wanted with that type of dreaming.

He went to the refrigerator next to the beer, wines and snacks. It all looked standard with no clues as to why Simone wanted him to come here. He walked around the bed and saw the flat screen that was on the right side of the bed. They hadn't watched a lot of television when they were here before, he remembered with a smile.

He walked past the bed and them went to the connecting bathroom. He saw the other robe and laughed at the memory of Simone yelling "three Jake, that's three robes! I'm going to wear all of them"

Jacob sat down on the bed and looked around.

"CeCe what are we doing here? What happened for us to even get here?"

The bell rang, and Jacob went to the door.

"Yes?"

"Delivery for Jacob."

Jacob relaxed and opened the door. Simone was standing there pushing a car. He stepped aside, and he closed the door. Before he could speak they, both heard it.

The barking of seals. Simone laughed. "See it doesn't matter if you are born rich or not those Seals set up shop like they belong and get to scare people thinking there are roving dogs on the loose."

"Cece why am I here?"

CHAPTER FORTY-NINE

John needed some space to finish this. Jacob had landed. It was time to get his insurance.

Underneath the gated community he had been tracking the underground network of gas pipes that ran throughout the community. He had loosened some safety features on the system and there were several slow leaks throughout the community. It was enough to set the alarms off.

John walked up to the young man at the Gate.

"Hi John" the young man called out.

John couldn't remember the man's name, so he just smiled and nodded.

"Say did you hear about the gas leaks that are showing up all around the community?" John said.

"No, did you tell Peter?"

"Peter left with the new people who came. They took Peter's car. But I called the services, so they could check it out."

The young man smiled "Good looking out. "

Sixteen minutes later, they both heard the sirens coming to the gateway.

The fireman came in their gear, looked at John and the young man before turning to John.

"Did you call in a leak?" the fireman asked.

"I did, you can follow me, and I can show you where I first smelled it." John said.

John walked toward the community center and the firemen asked him all the questions he knew they would.

"Has anyone reported any problems?"

"A couple of residents said they have nosebleeds."

"Has anyone reported having any other symptoms?" the fireman asked

"I think there was also someone complaining about their stomach." John said.

The fireman called over his shoulder. "Someone send for the inspector."

The fireman turned to John and asked. "Are the owners here?"

"No, but I have the security codes to give authorization to the community."

With a nod the fireman continued to go to the site and inspect the leak. It went like clockwork.

After the inspector came, John gave them the authorization codes and then they decided to evacuate a section of the property. It was in all of the safety manuals. The fire department couldn't identify a real cause or say there was anything above the normal parameters, but they didn't want to take any chances.

"Simple", thought John. Now the quarter that had Ms. Johns house was clear. He couldn't wait forever for them to come out. Now that the woman had turned off the cameras he needed to go in and John needed some space to finish this. Jacob had landed. It was time to get his insurance.

Underneath the gated community he had been tracking the underground network of gas pipes that ran throughout the community. He had loosened some safety features on the system and there were several slow leaks throughout the community. It was enough to set the alarms off.

John walked up to the young man at the Gate.

"Hi John" the young man called out.

John couldn't remember the man's name, so he just smiled and nodded.

"Say did you hear about the gas leaks that are showing up all around the community?" John said.

"No, did you tell Peter/"

'Peter left with the new people who came. They took Peter's car. But I called the services, so they could check it out."

The young man smiled "Good looking out. "

Sixteen minutes later, they both heard the sirens coming to the gateway.

The fireman came in their gear, looked at John and the young man before turning to John.

"Did you call in a leak?" the fireman asked.

"I did, you can follow me, and I can show you where I

first smelled it." John said.

John walked toward the community center and the firemen asked him all the questions he knew they would.

"Has anyone reported any problems?"

"A couple of residents said they have nosebleeds."

"Has anyone reported having any other symptoms?" the fireman asked

"I think there was also someone complaining about their stomach." John said.

The fireman called over his shoulder. "someone send for the inspector."

The fireman turned to John and asked. "Are the owners here?"

"No, but I have the security codes to give authorization to the community."

With a nod the fireman continued to go to the site and inspect the leak. It went like clockwork.

After the inspector came, John gave them the authorization codes and then they decided to evacuate a section of the property. It was in all of the safety manuals. The fire department couldn't identify a real cause or say there was anything above the normal parameters, but they didn't want to take any chances.

Simple John thought. Now the quarter that had Ms. Johns house was clear. He couldn't wait forever for them to come out and they were still moving around in the cold. He had initially decided to drop the temperature to make them more manageable but, Isabella was proving to be resourceful. Now that the woman had turned off the cameras he needed to go in and secure his property. The money or the code he didn't care which, but he was going to leave this property with one or the other.

Like all of his plans, it was simple.

CHAPTER FIFTY

Mr. Knight saw all the hustle and bustle going on. He knew this was the sign he had been waiting for. When the firemen came to him and asked him to leave, he flashed his badge and told him he was on business and would leave directly after. With a nod they went on their way.

He didn't know what was going on, but he knew if he left now he would miss his opportunity. The thing that caught his eye was the maintenance man. He was too helpful with the firemen. Knight knew he'd have to watch him a little closer.

It was all getting ready to come to a head and he wanted to be there when the end came.

CHAPTER FIFTY-ONE

Simone looked at the clean cut, rigid man that had once been her best friend. Before she could say a word, he started with the questions.

"Cece what are we doing here?"

The images of yesterday faded away and what was left was a stranger. The last time she'd seen him she'd accused him of bringing harm to David. He hadn't forgiven her for not telling him about David and she couldn't forgive him for talking to Sean. Now she could tell they were going to be polite for David's sake but nothing else. Jacob was all business.

"Really Jacob?" She walked towards him.

Jacob took a step back and Simone stopped in her tracks. Jacob's warm eyes were empty of everything. Here was the businessman who brought his efficiency to his clientele, not his feelings.

"Why are we here?"

Simone took the cover off of the bottom of the tray

and underneath there was a short stout briefcase. "Here's the money".

"Whose money?" Jacob asked.

"One of Sean's people will call you and then you can _ "

"Whose money is it CeCe?" Jacob demanded.

"It's the money that will save our child" she shouted back.

"I want to know why you are avoiding my question?"

"Jacob what do you want me to say?" Simone fired back.

"I want you to try the truth, what happened. I've heard everyone's take on this but yours."

"The only person you should trust is Peter."

"Does he know that you stole the money?"

Simone stopped and looked at him. She didn't deny it and Jacob swore.

Eventually Simone spoke.

"What would you like me to say oh great Jacob. Let me disappoint you, so you can stay on that high horse of yours. I own Safe Haven and the price for that was I would provide code to the other side when it was requested. I was selective about what I wanted to do. Then someone stole a project I was working on. They took it to market and sold it. They did it all under my name and my company."

"Do you know who?"

"If I had to take a guess I'd say it was Sean."

"Go on"

"I was already working with Mr. Knight so when this

problem arose they were more than happy to help me. They wanted me to give them whatever I had. Unfortunately, they weren't as upfront as they seemed either. I found someone who was at the selling of the software and found Mr. Knight was there too. It didn't help my trust issues with Mr. Knight. It was already pre-planned that I would die. I used the option early."

"Who was in the car?"

"Jacob, I don't ask the same questions. I do what I have to, to save David." She said exhausted

"I'm hoping if I ask at some point you'll start to care again. Simone it's for David can't be your answer to excuse whatever you do?'

"Yes, it can! You wouldn't understand that. You never did. I love my son. Like I loved you once. Love means sacrifice and it means there are no limits I won't go to."

Jacob walked up to her and held Simone to his chest. For a moment it was like the last time they were in this room together and then he pulled back and looked into her eyes.

"The problem with your type of love is you've already gone to the extreme of questionable behavior before your loved ones get in trouble. You might want to consider, you're the reason David is in this mess."

Simone pushed away from him and swung at him. Jacob caught her fist and the other in his hands.

"I tried it your way Jacob. I tried to do the right thing and it got me nowhere. Men took the credit for my work. I was a token at best to have on the team and only worth being someone's assistant. Not even a title Jake. I worked my ass off for two Assistant Directors and when they were promoted they took their Team leads with them." She said as she cried.

When the sobbing was over and there were only intermittent hiccups, Simone wiped her nose and straightened up.

"The contact will call you soon. Get ready." She said

"Do you have the code." Jacob asked.

"It's not here but it won't matter. I need to confirm who wants the money before I finish this."

"Simone, what are you doing? Why the long way only to have you bring the money?"

She laughed a hollow laugh. "I know you won't believe it but I'm protecting my son, the only way I know how. If this goes well then, we can argue later. If it doesn't don't cut Peter out of David's life. You may be a good man, but Peter is the man I want David to be, a realist."

"Why the cloak and dagger. You didn't need me here." Jacob said.

"I did Jacob. While they were watching you, they weren't watching me, Simone said"

Jacob's phone rang, Jane was on the other line.

"Did you find anything?"

"No code."

"And the money?" Simone was smiling at him as Jane spoke on the phone with that I told you so grin.

"I've got the money," Jacob replied.

"Bring it to the airport, your ticket will be there."

CHAPTER FIFTY-TWO

Options

"When you think about it, it's a modern-day marvel to see that much metal fly." Sean said to Mr. Knight.

"I'm sure you didn't bring me here to talk about planes." Mr. Knight replied.

"I brought you here for a couple of reasons, let's see how smart you government guys really are."

"Mr. Carstairs you contacted me, and I don't be having time for this." Knight said.

"I can see your accent gets a little thicker when you are feeling a little testy. You don't like this park?" Sean asked.

In front of the two men was a chain linked fence. On the other side of the fence were some weeds and then there was nothing but runways with several planes on them. There no trees to fend off the sun of midday.

"Get to the point Mr. Carstairs"

"The point is I'm at Plainview park because you are currently on a case here in New York. My office for your

information is in Orlando."

"Humph, you think you are the only one who has managed to get into the system. I'm not impressed Mr. Carstairs."

Sean laughed and held up his hand as he pointed to plane going down the runway.

"Did you see that Knight? It's an MD-80. Some will say that it shouldn't even be here on the runway. It's one of the old guard, gas guzzling jets. Some people consider it a technology deprived torture chamber in this day and age. That workhorse has been plagued by maintenance issues and still, it's a still a marvel"

Knight sat back on the bench and clapped his hands to get Sean's attention.

"Carstairs, I don't care two spits about the plane!"

"Oh Well, so much for appreciation. Let me see if I can enlighten you in some other way. I work for a company that makes software for Nova."

Knight sat up and looked at Sean.

"Oh, I see you know the company. Let me tell you what they are developing. They are making some program that basically can confuse the tower guys who help these planes get on and off the runway. When it's done it will be able to bring down planes anywhere in the U.S."

"Why you coming to me with this?"

"I want to offer you the first crack at this. I'm trying to be patriotic and let you buy it first as long as you don't insult me."

"I make no deals. Without a show and tell on your merchandise, you are just like every other crazy trying to get some cash."

"We will be giving a demo because we know how hard it is to trust these days."

"You'll build it and we'll get some kids to figure it out. It might not be as clean as yours, but they always do. What's tech today is nothing tomorrow."

Sean took a second look at Knight. "Maybe you're right. But, I think I can kill a lot of people before you get an answer."

Sean stood up. "This was a mistake. I was trying to offer you an opportunity and you want to play games."

Knight raised his hand. "I'm not blowing you off. But I won't be conned either. We'll buy what you're selling but, we'll have to see it in action."

Sean smiled. "I have one more thing to add to it. The developer of the product. She's not as open minded as we are. When I get the money, you'll handle her, I'll give you the product."

Knight nodded. "Done, if you can deliver."

Sean saluted Knight. "Nice doing business" then he walked away.

CHAPTER FIFTY-THREE

"Simone, Simone can you answer me? We don't have a lot of time David is sleep and I need to talk to you." Isabella said.

"I'm here."

"Tell me what the hell is going on! Is Jacob okay?"

"Jacob return. Jane money. Both return."

"You had the money and the code, and you put us all in danger." Isabella fumed.

"David first. Money acquired. Code mine.

Isabella hung her head in frustration. "We can argue later when this is over. What happens now?"

"Man, Knight good guy. Knight keep all safe."

"And Jacob?"

"Jacob fine. Called back up. Save Jacob. Danger on Sanctuary. Save David last resort give code, save David."

"Fine and Peter?"

"Peter understands."

"Fine, you take care of Jacob Simone and I'll take care of David."

Simone laughed on the other end. "Good guys no deals."

"We all have our pasts, I'm trying not to fall into mine."

CHAPTER FIFTY-FOUR

Sean arrived at the front desk of the Monterey Plaza hotel. He looked at the front desk clerks trying to derive which one to leave the message with. He walked up to the desk and spotted a person wearing a sign that said manager on duty. He stood at the counter and cleared his throat. The clerk turned.

"Can I help you," the clerk said from behind the counter.

"I need to leave a message."

"A message?" the clerk said warily.

"I have a message for the Spider."

The clerk grinned. "Ah yes, I take the messages for the widow. You don't look like the normal messenger, forgive me."

"I'm not sure if I should be happy about that or not." Sean said with a smile

"Do you need paper?"

Sean leaned on the counter. "I have a real problem. I

want to leave a message, but my issue is causing me a significant amount of money. Can you help me out? How long before the widow picks up the message?"

"There's no problem and no delay. The message can be retrieved immediately because the widow is in residence."

Sean almost jumped out of his seat. He needed to seem desperate but not pushy. "I'm really hard up here. I need to get an answer or I'm going to lose everything. I mean you probably hear that all the time but it's pretty bad."

The clerk contemplated Sean's words then said. "It says something if you let yourself get in the place. If you get help how long before you fall into this mess again. Is it really worth it to fix this maybe you should just walk away?"

Sean shook his head and hung it low. "You're probably right. I'm in a place that I never thought I'd be. I can wait. Thank you for your help."

Sean turned, and the clerk called out.

"Hold on." The clerk reached for a room key and handed it to him.

"Here, gives the widow your message yourself and good luck"

"Thank you" Sean said as he practically skipped to the elevators.

He rode the elevator up thinking about how to approach the Spider.

He walked along and found the room number. He waived his key over the lock and stepped in.

Then from his left Simone stepped out of the alcove and swung a large object toward his head. He tried to protect his head, but Sean wasn't fast enough and the next thing he saw was darkness.

* * *

Sean woke up and found himself tied to a chair. His arms were secured to the armrests and his ankles to the legs of the chair. In front of him was a coffee table and on the other side sat Roger and Simone.

"You've got to be kidding me." Sean spat.

"Hello Sean. Thank you so much for congratulating me on not being dead." Simone said.

"Oh Sean, I want you to know I've waited for a long time to see you like this." Roger said.

"I hope she's paying you well. With her reputation you probably won't live long enough to spend it." Sean said.

"No, I don't think you understand Sean, she didn't have to pay me. I did this for free." Roger said.

Sean thought they would do something to him. He took stock of his body and there was no pain.

"So, what's the plan? One of you plan on killing me? Simone, you have to know if I don't get in contact with my contact your son is dead. They are trapped in the house. If you let me go, I'll save David."

Simone laughed. "Oh Sean, you wouldn't know how to tell the truth if your life depended on it. Fortunately, it doesn't. I've put my own plans in place to take care of David. I just wanted you to come here to make sure you were far away, and I would have some leverage."

"Leverage?"

Roger cleared his throat. "Please let me Simone."

"You sent me to work in my own company. The company was bought by a certain person who also owns a boutique company on the web. He is the one you made a deal with. I've spoken to him and he wants one of three things."

Simone jumped up and down like a child. "Ask me, ask me"

Sean sneered at her. He was trying to control his breathing. Sean's brain was trying to process what he could offer or what he could do in order to get himself out of this.

"Speechless Sean," Simone said.

"My employer will take his money, the product or you. He's a simple man and he just wants to make sure that this predicament doesn't make him a target for other vendors."

Simone picked up her phone and texted Jacob:

'We've got Sean, get David and I'll meet you at the community.'

"I've texted Jacob. I've got to go. Roger, thank you."

"It's been a long road but I'm glad to have met you." Roger said to Simone.

"Well, I don't want you to take it the wrong way, but I hope we don't' meet again. I've got a child and one on the way. You are not the element they need to grow up around." Simone said.

"I know you Simone, good luck with keeping that "element" away." Roger said.

Simone walked out of the hotel room and Roger looked at Sean.

"I'll get comfortable, Sean. We are going to be here awhile, until my boss arrives"

CHAPTER FIFTY-FIVE

Deals with the Devil

"People usually run from the government, but I think there must be something in the water in Orlando because I keep getting invites from here." Knight answered.

Simone was sitting across from him in the booth. The diner was non-descript, but he wasn't here for the food. It was clear to Knight who the programmer that needed to be removed was.

"So, Ms. Johns, you invited me here, so why don't I let you begin."

Simone smiled. "I thought we would start the subterfuge a little later in the relationship but if you want it early, I'll accommodate."

Knight put down the plastic menu and raised an eyebrow at Simone.

Simeon was about to speak when the waiter came to take their order. The waiter was an older man who had a large paunch and an easy smile.

"Food?"

"Yes, we'll take whatever the lunch specials are." Simone said.

"Vegetarian or no?'

'Definitely no vegan."

The waiter smiled, and Simone turned to Knight.

"Where were we? Oh yes, we were at the point when I was surprised you were going to act coy about why we are meeting. Let me be clear Mr. Knight. I've had Sean followed. He met with you and then I had you followed. When your identity was confirmed I decided I should reach out to you."

"Mr. Carstairs, has already come and offered the product. We can't take possession of the product until we know it works. As to the dollar amount, if it can deliver on what it says then we will be very open to an amount."

"I have a question for you Mr. Knight? Do you think Sean is going to deal honestly with you?"

"I think that's a strange question to ask from a person who is betraying her partner."

"Partner? Is that what he told you we are?"

"It must be some sort of partnership for him to get the product, yes?"

"The issue I have with Sean is that he is not a partner. If he were he would have something vested. I own Safe Haven Inc. I've built a whole community from the employees and we live in Orlando. I'm sure you know. The issue is this company has some back-end funders. We provide specialized software in an exclusive market."

"Ms. Johns, you have a wonderful way of saying things."

Simone smiled. "thank you."

"At any rate recently I noticed someone had been stealing from my development lab. Usually it's not a big deal because the item is so big, or we have such a good handle on the release we don't' worry about corporate espionage."

The waiter came with the food and laid out the burgers and fries.

"In this case Sean was stealing the information from me. I know the leak isn't happening because they are breaking into the code, so it must be someone he has convinced to betray me. I keep moving the code and project and still I can tell someone is tripping the wire trying to look for it.

"Ms. Johns you could stop building."

"Mr. Knight this may be hard for you to understand but the reason I have the relationship with the funders on the code I write is because I need to push the envelope and make something that shouldn't be made. Usually I do it and then I throw it away."

"In this case you were building it and Sean stole it.

"Pretty much. I figured if I told them exactly what it could do I might be able to play it down, but Sean wasn't fooled. I found out the hard way he wasn't fooled and now I know he will be able to steal the finished product before I come up with a cure. I'm a patriot Mr. Knight. I know I don't fit the mold but, I want to deal. I'm always thinking America first. So, I'll give you the code when it's done.

"Do you have a price that goes with it." Mr. Knight asked.

"I do. I'll give you the code and you protect me, my son and Peter my lawyer."

Knight stopped eating and looked at Simone.

"It's not often that someone says something that surprises me but that did. No money, protective custody? Nothing else?"

"I can see how you thought I would be asking for more. We all do things for our own reason. I code and program because I like to solve puzzles and see how the answers can be applied everywhere. I have money and I have a family. I don't want to live in protection for the rest of my life either."

Knight waved his fork in the air. "I can't authorize this deal."

"Since Carstairs already gave his pitch I know he would have asked for money and knowing him my death. "

Knight sat back and wiped his mouth. "that was a good burger"

Simone had barely touched her burger. Knight on the other hand was done.

"The meal didn't agree with you Ms. Johns."

Simone smiled. "It's a bit hard to eat now. I'm very particular in my food selection."

"Well I'll eat for us. You build it and bring it to me; the government will take care of you and your sons need.

"Good. I disagree on selling anything that causes friction in my own county. Sean believes everything has a price."

"Is that your only reason." Knight asked.

"Sean isn't trustworthy and since my child that's a very important attribute."

CHAPTER FIFTY-SIX

Beginnings

"We are so up the creek without a paddle." Simone cried.

Peter just laughed at her. The both of them were in the bed trying to think this through. She was leaning on his shoulder and he was patting her on the back. When she realized his shaking shoulders had nothing to do with crying she pushed off of his chest and looked at him.

"Peter, we have a problem!"

"We do, I'm not denying it, but Simone you always say that saying when there is a problem."

"I do not"

"The first year when we found out one of the boutique companies had a person selling web supplies as additions to our software, you said we are so up the creek."

"Peter even you have to say that was so weird. I mean who wants to add malicious code to kiddie software."

Peter gathered her into his arms. "I'm not saying that the current situation isn't bad. It is but, we will find a way."

"I've been looking, Peter. I don't see the path out of this."

"First let's look at the facts."

Simone snuggled closer to Peter and pulled her floral print comforter to her chest. She remembered buying the comforter and Peter saying he'd never sleep under that many flowers unless he was dead but now here he was. So many things had changed and here she was at the moment when she had everything it was going to be taken away.

Simone sighed. "We know that no good Sean Carstairs has been stealing tech from Safe Haven, Inc. We also know that he has most of the code for the Houdini code. We know he's already sold it and the buyer has reached out to me saying he expects his code completed or he'll – "

"We don't know what he'll do so we have no facts." Peter interrupted. "We don't really know the buyer and we don't know what he will or won't do. We do know we have a weak link, David."

"David isn't a weak link! He's – "

Peter squeezed Simone. "Listen. If we didn't have David we might have some other options but, he changes things and our little one on the way." He said as he wrapped his hands around Simone's waist.

"Peter what are we going to do."

"We've already started doing what we can. We've made a deal with the government."

"A deal with them is only as good as it serves them."

"But it is a deal. We will continue to work with Sean and keep him as close as we can rather than isolating ourselves."

"When I see Sean I just want to kill him. If he were dead, this wouldn't be an issue."

"Is that what pregnancy does to a woman?" he joked.

"Ugh! I've killed him so many times the death scenes in my head are becoming repetitive." Simeon said.

"Concentrate. A deal with uncle SAM, tabs on Sean and an escape route for David."

"David, we haven't spoken about David."

Peter sighed. "What is there to say Simone. We agreed we'd do whatever it takes to take care of David. David first and you are second, that's what we agreed."

"Peter, I don't want to hurt you or our family and - "

"And what we agreed was Jacob Costa would die for his child."

"He would"

"Then we know he'd die for this child."

"Yes" Simone whispered.

"Good, because before this is over he may have to do that, and I want to make sure he doesn't flinch."

CHAPTER FIFTY-SEVEN

When Sean was unconscious on the floor Simone gave him another couple of kicks before Rogers walked into the room.

"Starting without me?" Rogers said.

Simone stopped and shook her head. "I was caught up in the heat of the moment. Tie him up and call your employer"

"Did you want me to tell him you got him here. Maybe he'll make a deal with you for David. -" The man said.

"I know you mean well Rogers, but these men only understand the black and white situations. You do this for your employer. I'm sure there will be some form of repayment."

Come on let me help you put him in a chair.

An hour later, they had Sean trussed up in a chair.

Simone patted Sean on the head. "You be a good puppy and stay. Roger call your employer. I have a plane to catch."

Rogers waited until she was gone before he made the call.

"Why are you calling me?" the simple man asked.

"Sir, I've acquired the seller." Roger said into his cell phone looking at Sean Carstairs sitting secured to a chair.

"Put me on speaker."

Roger put the phone on speaker and laid it down on the nearby coffee table.

"Mr. Carstairs, how are you?"

"I would be doing better if I wasn't tied to a chair by your employee. If you let me go I can get your product and your money."

"Is that true?"

"Yes, I don't know what Rogers has told you but me and him have history and it distorts his view. I am still working on getting your product."

"I am a simple man Mr. Carstairs."

Sean looked at Rogers who wouldn't look him in the face.

"I understand."

"I think we have been waiting for a very long time for the product. First you say you have it and then you say the coder died and stole it and now you say you think you have it again. For a simple man it seems like a lot of changes."

"I know it might seem odd, but I assure that – '

"Well, I guess that's the problem. I don't think I can take your assurances any more."

Sean started to stutter. "Please let me show you.'

"What will you show me exactly. Will you get the boy?"

"Yes! I'll – "

"I don't' need you for that. I'm about to get the boy myself. Maybe you could get the money?"

"Yes! Jane will – "

"Oh, I hope you're not talking about that sweet woman Jane. She's working for me and she's bringing my money to me. So, maybe you have the code?"

Sean looked around the room and then at Rogers.

"I-I don't have the product."

"That's a shame Mr. Carstairs because I don't have my product."

"Rogers hold him there. When I'm done I'll come visit to see what Sean can do for me."

"I could meet you and then – "

"No Mr. Carstarirs I'm a simple man. I want to finish this business and then I'll come and deal with that one."

The phone cut off and Sean looked at Rogers.

"He's the simple man."

Rogers nodded.

"I thought he was a made-up story."

"No, Sean, I wish he was."

CHAPTER FIFTY-EIGHT

Simone had given Jacob the money and stayed in the
hotel. She said she was going to see an old friend. He
didn't believe her but there was no time to argue with
Simone. Isabella and David were waiting.

Today was just not his day with women. Jacob had
received the text from Simone, when Jane showed up
behind him. With her fake smile and blond hair, she
grabbed the handle of the bag.

"Let it go or you won't be able to make it through
security." She said through clenched teeth. Jacob looked
around and figured it was a fifty-fifty bet to let it go. If
she tried to run, he could catch her and there were
enough cops around that he thought he could get
someone's attention.

He followed behind her as she went to the pre-check
line and their id was checked. When it was time to have
the bag scanned she looked at the three lanes and went
to a specific one. When the woman saw her coming and

244

waved her on, Jacob took a sigh of relief.

Jane had prepared for this. The woman got up from her seat and called a colleague over. The TSA agent then grabbed the bag and called Jane over.

"Ma'am follow me." Jane crooked her finger at Jacob. He was in the line next to her and had just finished passing through the body scan. When he saw her being pulled to the side he followed. At first one of the agents asked where he was going and then the female agent who was with Jane said he was to follow. He and Jane followed the agent to the side.

The women smiled at one another and then Jane opened the bag and the TSA agent took two stacks of money out of the bag.

The TSA agent nodded and then took a swab wiped the bag. Put the swab under a light next to the console and then smiled at Jane and said, "you can go."

Once they were on the way to the gate Jacob asked.

"She a friend of yours or a working buddy?"

"The simple man does business in a lot of places. Those are his friends. "Jane laughed and kept walking.

The plane loaded from front to back, so he saw Jane go by with the money in her hand. He didn't know how he was going to make it through this flight.

Jacob sat in his seat 85 million dollars lighter.

It was unreasonable but with that much money he had to make sure she and it were still on the plane.

With that much cash where would she put it, under the seat or in the overhead.

He wondered how Isabella was holding up. He

couldn't contact them, but he knew Isabella was an amazing woman. He had to keep his mind focused on what he knew not on what he couldn't control.

They boarded, and she took the bag. Jacob had 5 minutes to decide. He could text Bella and find out if they were okay or text Knight. He texted Knight.

"Blonde package on Southwest flight 162 with 85 million. Stop her."

He flexed his shoulders and waited for the passengers to finish boarding. The seat next to him was empty and any minute he expected to see who his neighbor would be. He closed his eyes for a moment and waited. The passengers kept passing and the number of children boarding slowed down the process even more. He reached above his head for the small air conditioner and turned it until he felt the stale air cool the sweat on his forehead.

Finally, the plane door closed and the gentle roll of the plane as it started down the runway. Jacob looked out of the window as the plane sped up until it defied gravity and took off. He was looking out the winding as the plane was banking to the left. When the plane straightened up the flight attendant came with refreshments. After her first pass Jacob was going to see Jane.

He got up to go to the coach section and the flight attendant smiled indulgently at him.

"Sir there is a bathroom behind you"

Jacob smiled back at her. "thank you, I know but my sister wasn't able to get first class tickets and I want to check on her. She wouldn't take my seat and I want to make sure she's okay."

The woman changed before him. What was once a flight attendant about to do battle with a stupid passenger became this nice grandma who patted Jacob on the back and said, "you go right ahead" in a soft conspiratorial tone.

Jacob found Jane in an exit row. When she saw him, she smiled.

"Are you checking up on me or the luggage?" She kicked the bag of money that was under the seat in front of her. He didn't answer and continued to walk to the back of the plane. When he walked past her again she had her eyes closed.

When he entered first class the attendant asked, "is all well?"

He nodded politely and went to the bathroom.

When he came out Jane was sitting in the seat next to his. When he stopped short the attendant patted him on the back.

"There's no one there, enjoy"

He sat down, and Jane waited until the attendants had disappeared into the secret sections of the front and the back of the plane.

"Thanks, big brother. I'm so grateful for you." Jane smiled at him and then pulled a blanket out to cover herself.

"Do you want to share a blanket/"

"No, I want my fiancée and my kid"

"Well, there's no accounting for taste. Soon enough

Jacob. You'll get what you deserve soon enough."

"Have you spoken to them.?"

"They weren't dead before we got on the plane."

"You've got your money."

"Yes, we do but we don't have the code." Jane said as she snuggled under the blanket.

"Neither do I"

"Everyone is saying that lately." Jane quipped.

Jane went to sleep, and Jacob looked out of the window.

"I'm coming Isabella, just hang in there" Jacob thought.

CHAPTER FIFTY-NINE

It was time to bring this to a close.

John knew his money was on a plane with Jane. Sean was in a hotel waiting for him to ask him some questions and there was a little boy in a house that would be the key to getting his product.

John took one of the golf carts he rode around the property in and went to the front gate. When he rolled up to the gate the young man was still there.

"Hey, I thought you would be leaving since they evacuated" John said to the boy.

"No, I want to wait and report directly to Peter and Isabella."

John nodded. "That's really good of you. I have some drink in the cart. Do you want some?"

The boy nodded. He stepped down out of the gatehouse and leaned into John's cart. John lifted his hand and then gave the injection of amytal to the boy's neck. The boy struggled for a moment, but John easily subdued him and put him in the cart.

When John got back to his house he threw the boy over his shoulder and then brought him in the house as he prepared to visit Isabella. John went to the spare room in the basement and turned towards the black monitors.

"Hello Housemates I have a surprise for you. This will be over very shortly. We need to meet in 2 hours in the front of the house."

"Sure, John we'd be happy to meet you. If you could open the door now, we'll get a late lunch and meet in what an hour." Isabella said sarcastically.

"You know Isabella, I'm going to miss you. I will be in the front of the house. I'll open the front door."

"What do you want?" Bella answered back.

"That's simple, I just want to exchange one boy for another."

CHAPTER SIXTY

As soon as the John had finished talking Peter and Isabella shared a look of desperation.

"Our time is running out." Peter said.

"Agreed" Isabella replied.

"I can see the back door to open. It leads to the garage and through the garage we can get to the community center. From there we can try to get one of the cars parked in the lot. There are keys located behind the front desk." Peter said.

"Okay, let's get David and Justice and go. Not that I'm not grateful but the question is if you could open the door all along why are we just leaving now." Isabella said.

"I'm not holding out on you Isabella. Simone made the suggestions when we were talking to her. I'm 80% sure it will work. While David was napping I was working on the door. I think I can get the locks to open

once but the safety gates will drop on all of the doors."
Peter said.

"Okay let's go." Isabella said.

They all traveled to the back door of the house. Justice
sniffed the bottom of the door and then looked back at
David. Peter stepped in front and spoke to the group.

"We need to move fast and quiet. If something
happens or if John is out there Isabella, you grab David
and run. Isabella, you know the plan. I'll catch up if
necessary, do we all understand?" Peter said.

He went to the door and pulled out what looked like
two small motherboards that could fit in his hand. They
were connected to a whiteboard, Isabella recognized as
a breadbox and it had been modified. With a USB
connector wire, he took the wire and positioned it under
the lock.

"Are we ready/"

Everyone nodded and then he said "go!"

Peter pushed the pin into the lock and then the light
on the door went green. They pushed through and
could hear the secondary safety gate falling. Isabella and
David were so close to him they all stumbled out onto
the floor. Justice cleared them by jumping over them
and then turned wagging her little tail as if they were
going to play the game again.

The gate fell down and they all sighed in relief. They
were in the back of the house they just had to get to the
garage.

"Help" David yelped. Isabella and Peter looked at
David thinking the worse, but it was just the cuff of his

jeans caught.

"Hold on baby" Isabella said, and she yanked his leg ripping the jeans.

"Let's get going" Peter urged.

* * *

John was already walking with his dazed gatekeeper to the house. When the buzz on the remote door lock in his pocket went off he dropped the man, gave a short yell of frustration and then grabbed the boy by his collar.

As he dragged the boy behind him he saw them on the floor. A man, a child and a woman.

"Stop, Stop now!" the simple man yelled.

* * *

Peter looked to his left and saw John coming.

"Get up and run!" Peter said

David got up with the adults and looked over his shoulder and then yanked his hand away Isabella'.

"It's my friend from the gate" David said confused

Peter and Bella both yelled for David to stop when he had cleared them, and he saw John pull a knife out and hold it to the young man's throat, David looked over his shoulder.

"Come here David" Peter called out.

'Listen baby come back to us" Isabella cried.

David took a step towards them and John yelled out.

"David if you don't come here I'm going to hurt your friend." John said with a smile. Then John took the knife and stabbed the man in the thigh. The young man screamed, and David trembled in the walkway.

"David come" Peter said as he tried to talk to him.

Isabella looked at the situation and knew John would kill the hostage and take David. The look in John's eyes was like a madman who had finally won. She turned to Justice with tears in her eyes.

"Jus' get David."

Isabella started running towards David when Justice took off. John yanked the blade out of the young man's thigh and then jabbed him in the throat. A splatter of blood decorated John's face and he threw the boy to the ground.

David was almost to his bleeding friend when the young man's body hit the ground. Just as John was going for David Justice jumped in the way.

"Get away you damn dog!" John tried to push off Justice and when that didn't work he stabbed Justice with the blade. Peter grabbed David in his arms and they were running back to the garage when Isabella heard the whimpers and growls from justice.

Isabella turned around with tears in her eyes.

"Jus' come. Stop baby and come!" Bella cried.

Justice relinquished her hold on John and tried to get to her feet.

Isabella could hear Peter calling her, but she couldn't move. She saw Justice on the floor and in that moment, she remembered.

Justice coming home for the first time. Jacob and her arguing about Justice in the bed and then she focused and saw Justice on the floor and ran towards her. She looked over her shoulder. "Go!"

Sanctuary of Lies

CHAPTER SIXTY-ONE

Jane wasn't as dumb as her blond hair suggested.

During the flight she stood up and pulled down the other bag down. The gentleman sitting next to her was a friendly sort.

"Excuse me. I have some personal items in this bag would you mind if I stored it under your seat, so I can reach it easier when we get off?" Jane asked.

He nodded, and Jane brought the bag down.

When the captain said they'd be landing in a few minutes Jane waited for the attendant to come with the garbage bag and got up towards the back. This would be tricky. The older attendant went to the back with Jane on her heels. She went to the bathroom door and saw the attendant putting the garbage in the cabinet. She stepped behind her and slammed her head against the cabinets. She slumped, and Jane had to make sure she didn't fall to the floor. She put her hip against her and lifted her body on to the seat and strapped her in.

One down and one to go. The other attendant was closer to her size. It wouldn't be an exact fit, but she'd have to make due. If she tried to exit the plane without a plan she'd be picked up right away. When the second attendant came the captain had already turned on the fasten your seatbelt sign.

"Miss, you have to take your seat we're landing." The attendant said impatiently.

"I'm so sorry I had to change my pad and - "

The attendant looked over Jane's shoulder and went to the slumped body. Jane didn't waste any time, with all of her force she slammed that attendant as well. The sound of the plane descending stopped anyone from looking back.

Jane changed into the other attendants close and then put one of them in the lavatory. She then opened her bag. Put on a black wig and pulled out a duster to throw over the outfit. As the plane hit the taxi she lingered. When the plane stopped she walked to the middle of the cabin. When the lights went on the passengers jockeyed for position. In the aisles. She gathered her bag and stood in line. Jane said goodbye to the attendant as she exited the plane. Then as she walked down the corridor she took off her duster and nodded to the authorities as she walked by. Jacob looked at her but didn't recognize her and she kept on walking.

＊ ＊ ＊

The plane was halfway emptied when Jacob received a call from Knight. Get to the property they're moving. The agent will bring you.

"Isabella?"

"I don't know but I know the property was evacuated by Ms. Johns house due to a gas leak. That's too much of a coincidence. "

Like clockwork an agent showed up saying Knight sent him.

"Where is Knight?" Jacob asked.

"He's on the property. He's sent for backup" the young officer told Jacob.

Jacob pulled his phone and called Isabella. The phone rang, and he let it go on ringing. He jumped into the car with the agent and sat in the seat waiting and hoping Isabella was keeping her wits about her and not letting her temper run amuck.

CHAPTER SIXTY-TWO

John raised his hand and ran towards Bella, with his knife ready to strike. Bella saw the knife but kept running towards him. When he swiped down at her she threw both of her hands up to catch his wrist then, she pulled her right knee up into his stomach. John grunted and punched her in the side with his other hand.

Isabella cried out but kept her grip on his wrist. Then she brought up her left knee into his kidney. His hand let the knife go and he started to fall, favoring his left. Before he could pull Isabella to the ground, she pushed her right hand up hitting him beneath his chin and clipping his head with her elbow. John's head popped back stunned for a moment. Instead of stopping him, it fueled his anger and he let out a roar of fury.

John let his body fall on Isabella and then he straddled her. He punched her once and she was dazed on the floor. She put her hands up to protect her face and tried to roll away, but he wouldn't let her escape.

"Why are you messing up the simple plan!", he yelled.

She picked up her legs and tried to kick him in the back of his head. He straightened up and grabbed the back of his head. Bella tried to buck him off of her. John braced himself from falling by throwing his hands out on both sides of her head and catching himself. Then he recovered and punched Bella one more time before she went still.

John heard the phone. He pushed himself off of Bella and patted her down until he got the phone from her pants pocket.

"Hello", he yelled.

"Bella?" Jacob asked.

"Bella's out cold now," John snickered through labored breathing.

"Who is this, where is David?" Jacob demanded.

"Ah, you must be Jacob. I've heard a lot about you. Do you have my product?"

"Where is Bella?'

"She's out cold and her dog too. Do you have my product?"

"I've got your money."

"So, no product. Bring my money and I might give you the boy."

John threw the phone to the floor and got up to follow the man and the boy.

* * *

David was crying in Peter's arms.

"Isabella! Jus! They're hurt. They're hurt. We have to

help! We have to- "

Peter kneeled in front of David and grabbed him by the shoulders.

"David listen. I will go back and help them but, I have to make sure the bad man doesn't get you."

David sniffed. "You're going to save Jus'"

Peter smiled. "I'll save Justice but now we have to go".

"Okay,"

"I don't think so" John said as he punched Peter from behind.

Peter fell to his knees and yelled. "David Run!"

Pain radiated through Peter's head as it popped back from the blow. In an instant Peter was back in prison. He rolled to the side and braced himself for the next blow. Peter reached out and kicked John bringing him to his knees. John tried to strike Peter but missed. Peter grabbed the arm and pulled him off balance. Peter scrambled to his feet, staggered from the lightheadedness he felt, righted himself and fell knee first on John.

John tried to block the incoming blows from Peter. Peter grabbed Johns arm by the elbow and then twisted it down until he heard the crunch of bone. John screamed in pain and tried to punch Peter with his other arm, but the blow had little strength behind it. Peter took two more punches until John was panting on the ground. He stood up and looked around for David.

John slowly sat up. "I want a lawyer."

Peter looked at him in disbelief. Blood poured from

Johns' face and his arm hung at an unnatural angle.

"I want a lawyer. This was all a mistake. I was paid to do a job." John said with a smile and blood dripping down his face.

"I want -" John's words were cut off when a bullet hole appeared dead center in his forehead. John's body fell back in slow motion.

Peter looked behind himself and there was Mr. Knight.

"I could see you were in mortal danger, Mr. Skiseng. You don't have to thank me." Mr. Knight said as he came closer.

Peter tried to take a step and look for David.

"Daddy, daddy!"

The last thing Peter saw was David coming towards him. Then it all went dark.

CHAPTER SIXTY-THREE

Peter opened his eyes and squinted against the bright glare of lights. He reached out and felt the cool metal railings. Simone was sitting in a chair next to his bed and David was in her arms.

In a moment it all came back to him. *Simone couldn't be here. He had to move them both.* He tried to sit up and the pain in his ribs made him wince and lay back down on the bed. He remembered the shots and then waking briefly in an ambulance and Simone barking orders like a general. Like a hawk she watched them and gave instructions on everything to how to put the I.V in, to what his blood type was.

"I knew Simone would do anything to be in the center of attention, so it shouldn't have surprised me that you were the same", Jacob said. Peter smiled and looked over to see Jacob and Isabella standing on his other side. Isabella had a bruise on her face and she was leaning against Jacob.

"Remind me never to piss you off." Peter said. *He remembered Justice.* Sorrow flooded him as he thought about her. "What about Justice?"

Isabella looked up at Jacob and then at him. "She's in recovery. The blade missed her major organs. She's not running yet but, she made it out of surgery and she was well enough to eat her favorite treats."

Peter looked at Simone. She smiled.

"To answer the other questions. John is dead. You kept calling for David and when I came in you calmed down, so I stayed. We have a deal with Mr. Knight. I will remain dead. You will be the executor of the company and on paper Jacob will be an owner of Safe Haven."

Peter looked at Isabella.

"And David?"

Simone answered. "I explained to David that he has two daddies. He says he has a friend who has two daddies, but they live together and sleep together. I told him you two are different."

Isabella laughed and put her hands on her ribs as the laugh caused her ribs to shake.

Jacob looked at Isabella and said, "See that is what you get for making fun of this situation."

"You all are a piece of work", Mr. Knight said as he entered Peter's room.

Peter fought off exhaustion to speak. "You had a deal with everybody. What kind of person does that?"

"A person who wants to win." Knight said "Look at things from my side, which is usually the bright side.

The bad guys, they be gone. The women be home and the children be sleep."

Isabella nodded towards him "and you be full of it."

A nurse came into the room and saw all the people.

"Badge or no badge you all need to leave but Simone and David. Peter is a big boy, but he needs to recover so out."

When they were all gone Simone looked into Peter's eyes.

"I thought I lost you," she said.

"What and disobey a direct command from the CEO of Safe haven," Peter replied

The former CEO" Simone said.

"I wouldn't leave our son," he said.

"I love you Peter."

"I love you too Simone and by the way, I want you to know when I was fighting John, NOW that was when it had all gone to hell in a handbasket."

"Whatever," Simone said as she rolled her eyes.

Simone leaned over and kissed Peter. "Get some rest so we can go home. This white room is driving me crazy."

Peter smiled and went to sleep. Tomorrow would be here soon enough, and he'd be able to go back to Sanctuary.

CHAPTER SIXTY-FOUR

Jane got off the bus.

She was dressed in old jeans and a peasant top. She walked down the road, past the light and a mile to the house. When she got there the boys were playing in the front and her sister was sitting on the porch sewing.

"Hello?" Jane called out. She wasn't even sure her sister would know her. Where Jane's hair was blond her sister's hair was brown. Where Jane was slim, her sister had the hips of a woman who had born children and the muscle of a woman who carried children on those hips.

"Come on up." Her sister called out.

"I thought I would stop by. I'm -"

"I know who you are. It's early you usually leave my package in the middle of the month. What's wrong, you in trouble? It seems like that is the only time people remember where their family lives."

All of a sudden Jane felt like she was a little girl again. Her sister had that same no-nonsense way of their mother.

"I need to rest my head. "Jane replied.

Jane waited for her sister to answer. Standing with her hands on her hips, she waited. If her sister told her to leave, she would.

"Come in. You look skinny like those city folks. This is your home too, so you're welcome. "her sister said.

Jane blinked back the tears and stepped onto the porch. The boys came to her.

"We didn't think you'd come home auntie. Grandma said you were just as stubborn as her, so you might not make it," the boys confessed to Jane.

"I told you all to be patient, right? I always told mama that you would wander a bit before you came home. Mama should have figured you'd be that way when she gave you that weird name. It made you want to travel, I guess?" Jane's sister answered.

"Yup, mama did say that all the time." the boys agreed nodding their heads.

"It's no matter I'm home now." Jane said

Her sister came out and asked. "You staying for dinner?"

"I'll stay for a spell if you don't mind?"

"Sarika, do what you want, you usually do."

* * * * *

HEADLINES: AIR TRAFFIC CONTROLLER
SUFFERED FROM SLEEP APNEA, NO CHARGES

www.ingramcontent.com/pod-product-compliance
Lightning Source LLC
Chambersburg PA
CBHW071131260626
47162CB00003B/750